I0760412

Nineteen Seventy-Six

THE SEVEN BOOK SIX

SARAH M. CRADIT

Copyright © 2019 Sarah M. Cradit

All rights reserved. This book or parts thereof may not be reproduced in any form, stored in any retrieval system, or transmitted in any form by any means—electronic, mechanical, photocopy, recording, or otherwise—without prior written permission of the publisher, except as provided by United States of America copyright law. For permission requests, write to the publisher, at "Attention: Permissions Coordinator," at the address below.

This is a work of fiction. Names, characters, places, and incidents either are the products of the author's imagination or are used fictitiously. Any resemblance to actual persons, living or dead, businesses, companies, events, or locales is entirely coincidental.

Cover Design by Sarah M. Cradit
Editing by Lawrence Editing

ISBN: 978-1-958744-29-1

Publisher Contact:
sarah@sarahmcradit.com
www.sarahmcradit.com

Preface

If you're here, you've hopefully started with *1970,* followed by *1972, 1973, 1974,* and *1975.*

1976 is a story that sets up storylines that have long-reaching effects, both in *The House of Crimson & Clover* and *Midnight Dynasty.* Some secrets will stay buried. Others have a way of revealing themselves.

One thing I feel compelled to point out, as I have in prior books: Although I mention *The House of Crimson & Clover* several times, it's not necessary to read that series to fully appreciate *The Seven.* I do, however, hope that when this series ends, it leaves you feeling the urge to see what happens next, for both these characters and their children. The Saga of Crimson & Clover is designed to have multiple ways of experiencing the world that never need to connect, unless you want them to, but I'll always hope I've done my job by making you want them to.

As with the earlier novels in the series, I feel it's important to add the disclaimer that I was not alive at any point in the '70s. I was raised on the music, values, and results of that period, coming up in the '80s with a vision of the world that matched what my parents had experienced in that pivotal decade. I've leveraged experiences and memories of those who did come of age in the era, but any errors are solely my own. If this paragraph looks familiar, you probably read a version of it in the Prefaces of the earlier books.

1976 is the penultimate installment in this series, and as this story begins barreling toward conclusion, I want to say thank you again for taking this journey with the seven.

Also by Sarah M. Cradit

KINGDOM OF THE WHITE SEA

Kingdom of the White Sea Trilogy

The Kingless Crown

The Broken Realm

The Hidden Kingdom

The Book of All Things

Blackwood Cycle

The Raven and the Rush

The Poison and the Paladin

Southerlands Cycle

The Sylvan and the Sand

The Flame and the Forsaken

Guardians Cycle

The Altruist and the Assassin

The Belle and the Blackbird

Darkwood Cycle

The Melody and the Master

The Hand and the Heart

Sceptre Cycle

The Claw and the Crowned

The Duke and the Disciple

THE SAGA OF CRIMSON & CLOVER

The House of Crimson and Clover Series

The Storm and the Darkness

Shattered

The Illusions of Eventide

Bound

Midnight Dynasty

Asunder

Empire of Shadows

Myths of Midwinter

The Hinterland Veil

The Secrets Amongst the Cypress

Within the Garden of Twilight

House of Dusk, House of Dawn

Midnight Dynasty Series

A Tempest of Discovery

A Storm of Revelations

A Torrent of Deceit

The Seven Series

Nineteen Seventy

Nineteen Seventy-Two

Nineteen Seventy-Three

Nineteen Seventy-Four

Nineteen Seventy-Five

Nineteen Seventy-Six

Nineteen Eighty

Vampires of the Merovingi Series

The Island

and more

The Dusk Trilogy

St. Charles at Dusk: The Story of Oz and Adrienne

Flourish: The Story of Anne Fontaine

Banshee: The Story of Giselle Deschanel

Crimson & Clover Stories

Available as a single collection, The Shorts

Surrender: The Story of Oz and Ana

Shame: The Story of Jonathan St. Andrews

Fire & Ice: The Story of Remy & Fleur

Dark Blessing: The Landry Triplets

Pandora's Box: The Story of Jasper & Pandora

The Menagerie: Oriana's Den of Iniquities

A Band of Heather: The Story of Colleen and Noah

The Ephemeral: The Story of Autumn & Gabriel

Bayou's Edge: The Landry Triplets

For more information, and exciting bonus material, visit www.sarahmcradit.com

The Seven in 1976

Children of
August Deschanel (deceased) &
Colleen "Irish Colleen" Brady

Charles August Deschanel, Aged 26
Augustus Charles Deschanel, Aged 25
Colleen Amelia Deschanel, Aged 24
Madeline Colleen Deschanel, Deceased
Evangeline Julianne Deschanel, Aged 22
Maureen Amelia Deschanel, Aged 20
Elizabeth Jeanne Deschanel, Aged 17

For Augustus

SPRING 1976

NEW ORLEANS, LOUISIANA
VACHERIE, LOUISIANA
CAMBRIDGE, MASSACHUSETTS

Prologue: Irish Colleen and the Seven

Colleen Deschanel, known as Irish Colleen to her family and friends, walked past the faces of her seven children, as she did every night of her life. Beside them now were pictures of her four grandchildren, all born within the past year: Olivia, Nicolas, Anasofiya, and, most recently, Amelia. More would come. She felt it. But four was more than enough for one year, especially the year their family had.

Word had reached Irish Colleen of Charles' illicit affair with the Sullivan girl. Almost half a year ago, according to the rumors, but if Irish Colleen knew about it, then so did most of New Orleans. So would the girl's husband, Colin, Charles' best, and maybe only real, friend. The rumors kicked up now, months after the crime, only because Catherine had gone missing. Fingers pointed at Charles, and tongues wagged without reprieve or clemency, and if Colin Sullivan *didn't* know about it, he was a fool, intentional or otherwise.

And now Charles was openly taking up with the French nanny Irish Colleen installed to help him with little Nicolas. Well, this wasn't the help she had in mind, and though it shouldn't surprise her that he wouldn't resist a young, beautiful woman, she'd hoped he had better sense than to keep all his problems brewing together under the same roof.

Augustus had taken three months off from work to look after his Anasofiya. If he mourned his dead wife, he didn't speak of it, or of her, at all. Only necessity brought him out of the house in those days. He'd sent for his groceries, and if anyone saw him outside of Magnolia Grace, it was walking Anasofiya in the fancy pram he'd bought to keep her safe from the harmful effects of the sun and other weather events that might appear at any time in the erratic springtime of New Orleans. He was a man devoted, but also, she knew, a man lost. Going back to work only worsened his fears.

Motherhood looked good on Colleen, now living at The Gardens, at least temporarily, with her husband, Noah. Amelia was born with a head full of shockingly white hair, with only the hint of soft gold. There were other Deschanels with these traits, Irish Colleen recalled from the old portraits, though almost none from the current generations. There was a Fontenot, maybe one of Eugenia's kids, but she couldn't remember their name. What mattered was that, for the very first time, Irish Colleen could enjoy not needing to worry about her oldest daughter's happiness. Though Colleen was mourning for her great aunt, for her brother's loss, she was managing through her grief because of Noah. Because of Amelia. Irish Colleen could rest easy, finally, where Colleen was concerned.

Irish Colleen still didn't quite know what to make of her quirky middle child. Evangeline seemed to be thriving in Massachusetts, at that technical college Augustus assured Irish Colleen was the best in the country. Leaving hadn't cured whatever ailed her; she was still this odd marriage of wild and cold; different. Other. She'd grown witty in her time away, and Irish Colleen thought Evangeline would be the type of woman she'd enjoy a card game with, over a bottle of wine, but this was her daughter, and she wanted more for her than to be the charming, single friend of all the married women.

Maureen's tempers had cooled, and she now invited Irish Colleen for lunch at her St. Charles home once a week. They talked mother-to-mother now, with Irish Colleen offering advice —rarely accepted—and funny anecdotes—always appreciated— over tea and whatever snacks Maureen's staff threw together. Maureen, her wild, imaginative child had always lived her life in the extremes, and for years, Irish Colleen worried this would lead her down a dark path. It did, for a spell, but Irish Colleen could see now that Maureen's obsessiveness could be a boon as much as a handicap. As a mother, she was utterly devoted. She'd found her purpose in Olivia.

Now, if only she could find a way to her husband.

Irish Colleen ascended the stairs, thinking of her grandbabies. She had so little to look after in her own life now, with Lizzy graduating in a couple months, and so she'd inserted herself into the world of her children's children. Always available and eager to babysit. A day without a baby in her arms was a sad day now, and she thought of this as she made her way to Elizabeth's room.

Connor, bless his heart, now at least pretended to sleep in the guest room. At least, until they thought she'd retired for the evening.

She found Elizabeth at her desk. The small lamp cast a glow over her paper and textbook, and the sound of her tapping her pencil against the wooden secretary echoed into the hall.

"Homework?"

"Studying for finals."

"Those are a ways away, though, aren't they?"

"I can test out now and graduate early."

Irish Colleen perched on the end of Elizabeth's bed, behind where her daughter sat. Elizabeth had asked to return to public school for her senior year, and though she'd never said why, Irish Colleen sussed it out one night, over cards and wine with the women who pretended to be her friends.

Connor couldn't take Elizabeth to prom unless they were both students at the same school.

"Why ever would you want to do that?"

"I hate school, that's why." Elizabeth sat back in her chair, gazing up. "Not *school* but, you know, *school school.*"

"It was your choice to go back to a public education, Lizzy."

"I didn't say it wasn't, Mother."

"Now I'm Mother? Not Mama?"

"Connor is trying to do the same thing," Elizabeth replied, ignoring the question, dodging the potential argument that lay behind the exchange. "He got accepted into Tulane. Did I tell you?"

"You did. How wonderful for him," Irish Colleen said. "But what about you? You haven't mentioned getting any college letters for yourself."

"I haven't gotten letters because I haven't applied to any."

Irish Colleen wrung her hands in the fold of her apron. She was not good at this. August would've been, but she was many years past thinking of what *he* would have done. "I don't know much about college, Liz, but shouldn't you have applied by now?"

"So now I'm Liz?"

"You're almost an adult."

Elizabeth set her pencil aside and stared toward the corner of her room. "I don't like it. Don't much like Lizzy either. I'll stick with Elizabeth, probably."

"But about the college applic—"

"I didn't miss the deadline," Elizabeth said. "Because, technically, there *isn't* a deadline if you don't intend to go."

"Don't intend... Elizabeth, seriously? Not go?" Irish Colleen was incredulous.

"You get all bent about Evie going away to study science, and then get twisted about me not wanting to go at all, so which is it? Is school good or bad? Does it make our lives better, or is it silly, just a waste for a woman when she could have a husband and kids to look after?"

Irish Colleen balked. "That's not fair. I fully support Evangeline's decision. I just wish she'd *talk* to me, is all. She's always so brooding and cynical, and I never know what's on her mind."

Elizabeth spun her chair around to face her mother. "No one owes you access to their thoughts. Not everyone likes to share."

"You used to."

Elizabeth made a dramatic glance at the calendar. "Oh, yes, it's spring. Time for your annual soothsaying, is that it? If I tell you what I've seen, will you let me get to bed?"

"You weren't even in bed when I came in!"

"Not the point."

"What's gotten into you?"

"No deaths, at least that I've seen," Elizabeth said flippantly, yawning in the middle of the sentence. "Good thing we're rich, though."

"What is going on with you?"

"Gonna need all the moolah in the bank to pay for the therapy everyone's going to need before this year's up."

CHAPTER 1

But, What if You Could?

Augustus' alarm went off, but it needn't have bothered. Setting it was only a habit now, not a necessity. He wasn't asleep. He remembered every last creak of the house settling throughout the long night; every change in the pace or pitch of Anasofiya's breathing. If he'd slept at all, it hadn't been for long.

He was getting used to this now. It was okay. He didn't need sleep, not if being awake meant being vigilant to his daughter's well-being. Irish Colleen might chide him for keeping the bassinet in his room, but when her children were babies, there were two parents in the home. Double the security, in the event of an emergency, and for an infant, emergencies lurked around every corner.

It could be disruptive to her sleep as well, darling, not just yours.

I let her sleep, Mama. I only go to her when she wakes up.

You should only go to her if she's hungry or needs changing, Augustus. You'll spoil her like this, training her to know how easily it is to wrap Daddy around her finger.

"I'd rather her wrap me around her little fingers than ever worry that her daddy isn't there," Augustus whispered as he lifted his little redheaded beauty into his arms, careful to support her developing head and neck. "Ready to eat? We just had a delivery of milk only yesterday. Your wet nurse is on the ball."

He'd considered installing an elevator, to avoid the prospective disaster of him losing his footing as he carried Ana down the stairs. The steel housing was there, from the early twentieth century, when Magnolia Grace *had* been equipped with one, but when one of the little cousins got trapped in there for two days, August had the thing removed, and a wall put up.

"You're up," Elizabeth called from the kitchen. She sat hunched over a bowl of cereal, scooping her spoonfuls like a caveman. Often, she and Connor stayed over now, though Augustus hadn't asked. In the morning, Irish Colleen would show up and they'd pass one another like the changing of the guard, which was probably how they saw their presence in his life, Augustus realized.

"You're here," he charged, switching Ana to the other arm.

"I made her a bottle," Elizabeth replied without looking up from her food. "It's on the warmer."

"Thank you," he said. "But that wasn't necessary. I can do it."

"I know you *can* do it, Aggie. I decided to be helpful, since I was up."

"Where's Connor?"

Elizabeth glanced up at the clock that hung over the door. She groaned. "About to be late for school if he doesn't get his ass out of bed."

Augustus settled a dishrag over his pajamas and rotated his daughter to a better position to feed her. Ana latched on to the nipple of the bottle immediately, sucking hungrily. He released the breath he'd been holding; the one attached to his fear she'd stop eating, stop trying, stop living, just like her mother. "You don't have to stay here. I've got everything under control."

"Oh yeah? That why you were up all night long?"

Augustus swiveled the bottle higher so Ana could have better access. "Most parents don't sleep when their babies are young."

"Most parents aren't shy about asking for help when they

need it."

"When they need it," Augustus emphasized.

Elizabeth dropped the spoon into her empty bowl with a loud clang. "You going to work today?"

"Why wouldn't I?"

Elizabeth rinsed her bowl without using soap and dropped it in the dish rack. One more thing he'd have to attend to later. "I guess I should be asking, are you going to *stay* at work?"

Augustus ignored this question. Instead, he breathed in the soft, baby scent of Anasofiya's hair as she drank her breakfast. Real. She was real. Alive.

"That'll be Mama," Elizabeth said when the bell rang.

Rory and Carolina's apartment was lovely, modestly appointed but sumptuously located around the inner edge of the bustling green of Boston Common, now in full bloom for spring. They were high enough to have some privacy, while still overlooking the flurry of activity in the heartbeat of Boston.

Colleen noted the apartment had three bedrooms, an important detail that would matter later if she was successful in her plea.

A sinking sensation ebbed and flowed through her, as she thought of Evangeline, mere miles away, oblivious to the fact Colleen was in the area at all. It would be so easy to call her for a lunch date, or to stay at her small apartment in Cambridge and catch up into the early morning hours.

But she had more pressing matters here, and to explain them to Evangeline, no matter how bad she might want to, was out of the question. This wasn't her secret to share outside of the people required to know to enact the proper plan. Her only motivation for telling Evangeline would be to have someone to confide in, and that wasn't good enough to bring someone else into the already convoluted affair.

Clancy was big enough to run around on the shag carpet, while spouting off quite a few words, stringing together a handful of complete sentences. He was a lovely toddler, a head of soft blond tufts, eyes full of muted mischief.

Before revealing the intent of her visit, Colleen muddled through the required pleasantries and catching up. Rory did well enough to hide his surprise at Colleen's quick marriage, but was less effective at burying his shock when learning about her daughter, Amelia. He said, with a light sting of accusation, that Colleen had forgotten there were people who loved her; people who might want to know about the major events altering her life. In crafting her new life in Scotland, it hadn't only been Colleen's family who were left in the dark.

Carolina's reaction was appropriately tender. She seemed well past whatever jealousy or fear she had toward Colleen, where her husband was concerned, and that left Colleen's heart happy. The couple's body language strongly indicated their closeness and there was something even more powerful in the glances cast on one another when the other wasn't looking. Rory and Carolina's marriage may have begun for the wrong reasons, but, either through the strife of Clancy's hard birth, or something else, something Colleen may never be privy to, had forged into something far more impenetrable and meaningful.

They were both eager to meet Amelia, and Colleen wished, briefly, she'd brought her on this trip. But it was better to leave her in New Orleans with Irish Colleen, so Colleen could focus all her attention on the task at hand.

It was only two days, after all, though two days felt an eternity when her heart was thousands of miles away.

Well, half her heart. The other half sat at her side, prepared to do anything he needed to help her achieve her goal. Several lives depended on their power to convince Rory and Carolina.

When they asked when she'd start going by Colleen Jameson, she explained that her name was already changed on all official paperwork, but that publicly, when representing her family, she would always go by Colleen Deschanel. When she'd learned this was a requirement of any magistrate of the Deschanel Collective

Council—something Ophelia never had to contend with, having never married—Colleen initially feared this might be a point of contention in her young marriage. But Noah was delightfully understanding. He knew what their marriage license read, he said. He knew who *they* were.

Noah and Rory hit it off right away, and Colleen realized, somewhere in the midst of them reciting current sports team rankings in New Orleans, and reminiscing about old haunts unfamiliar to her, that the world of the Jamesons and Sullivans had been more tightly knit to one another than the Deschanels had been to either of them. The Sullivans might today live comfortably amongst the blue bloods, but they'd started as blue collar men with big dreams, and their clients, and the city, embraced their proletarian roots as proof of what hard work and a vision could produce.

Carolina set a tray of lemonade on the coffee table. She disappeared into the other room for a moment, and when she came back, the pitched sound of cartoons—*The Flintstones*—followed by Clancy's squeal, replaced the silence.

"So," Carolina began, a careful smile hardening her soft features. "You said you had something important to talk to us about?"

Colleen and Noah exchanged wary glances. Time was running short, if this plan was to work.

"Something has happened back home," Colleen began. "Something... requiring your full discretion, regardless of what you decide here today."

"Of course," Rory insisted, Carolina nodding at his side. "You know you can always trust in our discretion."

"Yes, I know," Colleen said. "But this particular situation involves your brother."

Rory's eyes twitched. "Which one?"

"Colin."

He appeared surprised. "Colin? Colin's in trouble?"

"He could be. It's not something he did," Colleen added

quickly. "But it affects him directly, and he must never know about this. Ever." She looked at both her old friends, one by one. "I mean it. If you tell me to go fly a kite, you still can *never* repeat what I'm about to tell you. I'm taking a huge risk, on someone else's behalf, even in coming here."

"When have I ever told you to go fly a kite?" Rory asked.

"Colleen, I don't like where this is going," Carolina said as she poured them each a glass of her homemade lemonade.

"But do you promise?"

"Yes, but—"

"No, Car. There is no 'but' here. You either promise, or you don't. If you don't, Noah and I will take you out to dinner tonight, and we can catch up on our lives and enjoy the rest of our visit as old friends making up for lost time. But I can't tell you what I'm about to say without your utmost vow of secrecy."

"Jesus," Rory whispered. "Is it that bad?"

"Do you promise?"

He looked ready to rebut again, but instead nodded. "Yes, I promise."

"Carolina?"

"Yes... yes, I suppose. I promise."

"It's only bad," Colleen answered, satisfied in their faithfulness, "if there's no solution."

CHARLES GROANED AS THE ORGASM LEFT HIS BODY IN A series of shuddering spurts. Lisette smiled evenly and waited for him to completely finish before rolling out of bed, sheet wrapped around her tiny, lithe body, and heading to the bathroom to clean herself up.

If he didn't know better, he'd think their sex had become more dutiful than passionate from her end, but he did know better. She loved him, as much as he loved her. How could she not?

"I will check later for pregnancy," she called from the bathroom. The toilet flushed. "Charles? You hear?"

"Yes, I hear!" he called back, frowning into the pillow. He didn't like the way she talked about their future child, like he or she was a business transaction and not a beautiful life, binding their little family together and making it ever more real. "But you just checked yesterday. It's not too soon?"

"Never too soon," Lisette said, appearing in the doorway, now fully clothed. So much for a second round. Last time he'd tried to proposition her after she was all cleaned up, she'd told him only animals couldn't control themselves. "You want a baby. I want to give you happy news."

"*We* want a baby," he reminded her.

Lisette reached for the clip on the dresser, the one that held her hair back so Nicolas couldn't rip at it with his strong fists. "Nicolas needs me."

"I can go to him."

"No," she said, securing the clip. "My job."

Charles licked his lips and rolled back in the bed, exposing what used to be a chiseled chest, in his heyday. "I have another job for you."

The impatience that flashed across her eyes wounded him. Like he was a child, no different than her charge. "Later. I promise."

"I love you," he called, but she was already gone.

Charles turned to the clock. Nine already. Colin would be here soon. He wished there were a delicate way to turn his friend down, but there wasn't, not with circumstances what they were now, with Catherine ignoring her husband's calls; his pleas to see her, or their son.

Catherine.

Always fucking Catherine.

Colleen explained all she knew about the situation, which was less than she would've liked, playing the role of problem solver. She told them that the marriage between Colin and Catherine, according to the latter, had been on thin ice since the birth of Oz. That the differences always existing between them grew wider and more pronounced, with Colin throwing himself deeper into his work, and Catherine seeking validation elsewhere.

Namely, with Charles.

Rory's and Carolina's faces paled as the story unfolded.

The affair, according to Catherine, lasted months, and by the time Charles broke it off, it was already too late to go on as if nothing had happened. Catherine hadn't visited a doctor, because she didn't believe there were any in New Orleans who would keep her counsel without telling either her husband or her lover, but based on how she was showing, when compared to her pregnancy with Oz, she believed she'd become pregnant around the second month of their tryst.

No, Colleen told them, there was no chance this baby was Colin's.

No, Charles didn't know. Could never know, just as Colin couldn't.

"And soon," she said, as she came to the end of everything she knew, "she won't be able to hide it anymore."

Rory looked away from them, out the window. His face was unreadable, but his body was tense. "Who else knows?"

"The four of us," Colleen answered. "Catherine is currently staying with her mother, but she can't for much longer. Her mother may already suspect, but soon it will be a lot more than a suspicion."

"But she's her mother! If I were in trouble, that's who I'd turn to," Carolina retorted. She looked at her husband. "Or you, of course, dear."

"Your mother isn't her mother," Noah said. "She has her reasons, and whatever they are, we're past that. Catherine approached Colleen for help because she's out of options."

"I didn't realize the two of you were friends," said Rory, in a tone bordering on accusatory.

"We're not," Colleen replied. She wrapped one hand around her empty belly, a habit she'd grown so used to that she now missed. She crossed her legs, one foot dangling, tapping the air. "I never approved of her relationship with Huck, even before she married your brother. You might remember that."

Rory looked off to the side.

"She came to me, she said, because she sees me as a problem solver."

"I can see that," said Carolina, nodding. She craned her neck to listen for Clancy in the other room, but there was nothing but the action of the cartoon show.

"And how do you plan to solve *this* problem, Colleen?" Rory asked. He sounded almost amused. "Jesus," he added, under his breath. "Jesus H. Christ. Colin would die if he ever found out. His heart would up and fail."

"We agree," Colleen said. She turned to Noah, who gave her a tight, encouraging smile. "That's why we're here."

"We'll help however we can," Carolina said. She looked at Rory for support, but he'd gone somewhere else entirely, staring off into the corner with an intense look. "But short of magic, I don't know how. We can't turn back time."

"She's too far along to... ah, I hate to even suggest it—"

"Then don't, darling," Carolina said, voice hard. Sweeter, she said to Colleen, "You seem to have a plan in mind."

"When I saw you both last, you said you wanted more children." Colleen's heart leapt forward into a dead sprint. No matter how many times she'd practiced this conversation in her mind, she knew it wouldn't ever compare to saying it aloud. If she couldn't convince them, then she had no backup plan for Catherine.

"We can't have more children," Carolina replied, peering down at her fingers, laced together across her emerald polyester skirt.

Colleen took a deep breath. "But what if you could?"

Over the next thirty minutes, Colleen laid out, through the meticulous choice of words and phrases, her proposal.

If they agreed, Catherine would fly to Boston immediately and take up residence in their third room, which was currently only occupied by Carolina's sewing projects. Oz would come as well, or it would look as if she'd abandoned her son, which would raise far more suspicion. She'd stay there until she gave birth, and likely for a couple weeks after, to recover. During this time, Catherine would remain separated from Colin. By the time she returned to New Orleans with Oz, he'd have no indication she was ever even pregnant, and if reconciliation was in the cards, he'd never be the wiser.

Her child would remain in Boston with her new family.

"A daughter," Colleen said, knowing how bad Carolina wanted a little girl, and using it without hesitation. She could be angry at herself for the blatant manipulation later. "I laid hands on her."

Carolina and Rory would raise Catherine's little girl as their own, Colleen promised. No one would ever know Carolina wasn't pregnant; their life away in Boston provided the perfect foil for doubters, and her problems with the last pregnancy would easily explain why they'd kept the news to themselves until they were certain all was okay.

The secret would remain between only those in possession of the knowledge today.

At first they said no.

Then they asked if they could think about it.

Colleen said they had until she and Noah flew back to New Orleans in the morning. But if they did not want to parent this little girl, she was racing a clock to find someone who would.

If they raised this child, she said, she would live among Sullivans, where Catherine could, maybe one day, see her again. The child may not be Colin's, but were the Deschanels and Sullivans not also family, where it mattered?

"If we do this..." Carolina paused, overcome by emotion.

"We should talk, Car," Rory said. "We can't just commit to something like this."

Carolina ignored him. "If we do this, we need a guarantee Catherine won't change her mind later."

Colleen looked at Rory. "You can draw up paperwork that assures this, yes? You know what to put in it? To protect yourselves?"

He sucked in his lower lip, followed by a single nod.

"What role would Catherine expect in her daughter's life, exactly?" Carolina asked.

"*Your* daughter's life," Colleen corrected. She didn't dare look at Noah. This had worked. She felt it, even if the agreement was still in the future. "She would be Aunt Cat, just as she is to Clancy. Nothing more, or less."

"Catherine seems to believe fixing her marriage is in her best interest," Noah added. He'd said little, respecting that this was Colleen's show, not his. She loved him for that, and for knowing when to jump in and support her. "For her, and her son. Bringing home a love child wouldn't make that very easy, I'm sure." He chuckled, but it came out like a cough. "The alternative is her little one ends up with a stranger."

"As a mother now myself," Colleen said, struggling through the words as her imagination allowed her to stand in Catherine's shoes, "I can't imagine the pain of seeing a child of mine with a stranger, not when there was a better way."

"That's what most people do when they have an unwanted baby," Rory said.

"But this baby isn't unwanted," Colleen pressed gently. "Is she?"

Carolina dropped her eyes to her lap. Tears dotted her cheeks. Rory squeezed her hand and sighed.

"No," he said, eyes fixed on his wife, who had endured so much to bring a child into their life. "I suppose not."

"A CHILD NEEDS A MATERNAL INFLUENCE," IRISH Colleen said. She'd tried three times to take Anasofiya into her arms and failed each when Augustus dodged her attempts.

"A child needs her parents, and my daughter, unfortunately, has only one."

"Augustus." Irish Colleen tugged at her apron as if searching for her famous patience. "There is no shame in a nanny. None."

Augustus bounced Anasofiya on his shoulder. *Come on. Burp already. Please, Ana. Don't make yourself sick.* "You never used one."

Irish Colleen's hands flew to her hips. So much for patience. "I never used one, because my children had both a mother *and* a father! Son, you're a wonderful man, and a great father. But how can you, the most honorable man I know, not understand how your little girl needs a woman in her life?"

"She has you," Augustus said. He turned away as he patted Ana's back in growing anxiousness. If she didn't burp... *no, don't think it.* "Lizzy. Maureen. Colleen."

"You won't even let me hold her."

"You can hold her when I leave."

"It's nearly ten, Augustus. Just when did you plan on leaving?"

Ana made a light gurgling noise as she expelled the excess of her breakfast. His heart rate slowed. They'd made it through another morning. Safe. Sound.

"Here," he said, handing his daughter to his mother with great reluctance. "See? You're holding her." He shoved his shaking hands in his pajama pants. Pajamas. He wasn't even dressed. Maybe he should stay home today, since it was already so late.

"You can hardly stand to see me do it."

"You're my mother," Augustus said, but this was no answer.

"I am your mother," she said, taking Anasofiya so naturally into her arms that Augustus felt a pang of failure at his own awkwardness. "And as your mother, I'm going to tell you something that will be hard for both of us."

Augustus stared at her.

"You need help, son."

CHAPTER 2
How Very

She's not at her Mom's, Huck. Not anymore. No one knows where she and Oz are. She said she needed time and then... then she disappeared. With my son.

With my son, Charles.

Charles had been cagey with Colin on his quest to bring his wife home. After the day he'd given him advice in the form of tough love, he'd switched to listening, because he knew anything he said would be unhelpful with Colin so upset.

But that was before Catherine went missing. Before she'd taken her son and disappeared.

If Cordelia ever took his son and vanished, Charles would murder her with his own hands when he found her. The last thing she'd see would be her own regret as he strangled the life out of her, slowly.

He wanted to murder Catherine for doing it to his best friend.

Some lines should never be crossed.

Charles drove. Colin hunkered in the passenger seat, chewing his pristine nails as he focused on the things outside the window.

. . .

Colleen wanted this meeting to be over. She wanted to leave the chambers and disappear into the magistrate's residence suite of The Gardens, where her husband and daughter awaited. Snuggling with her two loves was night and day more appealing than listening to the Council dress her down for her first official decision as magistrate.

They couldn't say she didn't offer them the opportunity to weigh in. It was Pierce who'd reminded her that the decision to pick the seventh Council member was hers and hers alone. She offered them all a say, and they turned her down, for tradition.

Now, they were questioning both her decision *and* the tradition.

Colleen focused hard to push her ache for the wisdom of Ophelia into the back of her mind, where it now belonged.

"If I'd picked a Deschanel, you'd chide me for that, despite that I'm the only one on the Council today," Colleen defended. "So I picked a Fontenot." She nodded at Eugenia. "*Your* son."

"He's fourteen, Colleen," Pierce said. "Fourteen. We don't even allow Collective *members* at fourteen, let alone on the Council. What message will this send?"

Colleen again turned to Eugenia. "Do you think Luther is too immature for this responsibility?"

"His maturity isn't an issue," Eugenia said carefully. What was she thinking? Did she support Colleen's choice? And if she did, would she back her in this group, or side with the majority and team up on her?

"Is there any issue, Eugenia, that you can think of?"

Eugenia glanced at her brothers, Pierce and Cassius. "Other than his age, no."

"Other than his age," Colleen repeated. "Well, you're his mother, and he's not yet old enough to make decisions for himself, even by our rules." Eugenia might hate her for this next part, but it had to be done. She couldn't be the only one on the Council with a horse in this race, and if Eugenia fell in line, the others would. They'd always deferred to her. She should've been magistrate; Ophelia shouldn't have passed her over, creating this rift. "I need your blessing, in this case, so I leave the decision to you."

Eugenia's eyes twitched, ready to narrow. She kept her composure. "It isn't my decision to make."

"Without your permission I can't bring Luther in, at his age, so, unfortunately, it is."

"I don't like this," Cassius muttered.

Colleen ignored him and continued to wait for Eugenia's reply.

"It would be unfair of me to deny him this opportunity," Eugenia began, with caution. "But if I say he can, then I take the responsibility from you, which is also unfair."

"Shall I find another candidate?"

Eugenia huffed and looked away. "Do whatever you want, Colleen. I won't hold my own son back."

This was going all wrong. Colleen was damned if she did, and damned if she didn't. Had she chosen Evangeline—her top pick—they would've skewered her for picking favorites, despite that Colleen was the only Council member from the line of August. So she ignored the fact they already had five of Blanche's brood and dipped her feelers to that side of the family—again. All of Blanche's children were already Council members, so that left the younger generation, and of them—aside from Pansy and Kitty, who were already on the Council—only Luther was competent enough to overcome the hardship of his young age. She liked him; though only a freshman in high school, he was smart, focused, and almost too serious for a young man his age. Colleen saw a bit of herself reflected in Luther Fontenot, and, maybe, an ally.

"Look," Colleen went on, trying to shift the tension back to spirited discussion. "I'm not trying to create trouble between all of us. I did consider a Deschanel. Evangeline, if you want to know, and I think, I *hope* one day, she will be sitting here with us. But the timing was wrong, and besides, the last thing I wanted was for all of you to look at me and see my first decision being, in your eyes, an act of nepotism."

Cassius and Eugenia both cast their eyes away. Pierce picked at his fingernails, and Kitty scribbled furiously in her notebook.

Only Pansy met her gaze. "Colleen, you can't win in a game that was never designed for you to win. Ophelia is the only one of us, in *this* country, to ever hold the magistrate role, and while we all know Ophelia is a *queen,* she ain't the only one capable of steering this ship. She chose ya for a reason, cousin. We gotta respect that." She looked at her father, sister, aunt, uncle. "We *do* respect that. Evangeline would make a fine member. So would Luther, even if he is young. But he ain't the youngest, and if we're gonna make a world for our kids, we gotta let them into it, too."

Colleen listened gratefully. Pansy was the most unlikely ally she could think of in this room. Colleen suspected she'd never liked her, for one, and, like her mother, Pansy was headstrong and wasn't much for the dust and cobwebs of tradition.

"Pansy is right," Cassius said, another strange bedfellow. Colleen always suspected Pansy and Cassius to be the two least likely to support her, but so much else had changed, so why not this, too? "We can't tell you to make a choice and then pick it apart. Ophelia has only been in her grave a few months, and we dishonor her with this infighting. It has to stop." He looked at Colleen. "She chose you for a reason. You have my support."

Pierce nodded for a few seconds, choosing his words. "Maybe this is *why* she picked you, Colleen. We all liked to think of Ophelia as old guard, but I remember her listening to your new ideas, about science and discovery, and let's not forget she could see the future."

Others nodded.

"*All* of it," Pierce went on, and several laughed. Colleen folded her hands in her lap, unsure of where this was going, but no longer anxious. "So, surely, she saw you picking Luther? Right? And if she thought this decision was problematic, would she have chosen you?"

"You can't change the future," Eugenia countered. "No one knew that better than Tante Ophelia."

"No," he agreed. "But that doesn't mean she didn't endorse it."

"Frankly, I don't even know why this ancient tradition still exists," Kitty offered. "The Collective. The Council. We meet every quarter to talk about *nothing*. When's the last time we even pulled the broader Collective in for a meeting?"

"The Collective meets annually, or when there's a need," Colleen reminded her. "The tradition isn't designed for them to be a constant part of things."

"Our annual numbers last year were..." Kitty flipped through her notebook, consulting her fastidious record keeping. "Twenty-two. We had twenty-two people show up for the annual briefing. That twenty-two includes us, by the way, so fifteen. And why? Because there's never anything to discuss."

"Until there is," Colleen said.

"Until there is," Cassius parroted. "Ophelia revived this old tradition from our French ancestors for a reason. Things weren't always so peaceful for us. Most of us weren't alive the last time the Deschanel Curse swept through the family. We should be happy that our problems are that of a normal family, and not of the magical persuasion. But one day, they will be. History is cyclical. We've been in a period of peace for far too long, and we all know it. Ophelia knew it. She spent her whole life warning us of it and was the only one who never forgot where we came from, and why this"—he gestured around the table, at the ancestral portraits, the wall sconces—"was necessary."

"Amen, Uncle," Pansy said, head lowered, hand in the air.

"We're way off topic at this point," Colleen said. "Here's the thing, everyone. It may be my decision, but as my first decision, in what will be a long line of them seeing as this role has the longevity of a Supreme Court justice, I don't want this to create a divide. I *care* what you all think. I do. So, I'm making the decision to put it to vote. We'll go with a simple majority, though I'll sleep better if the verdict is unanimous."

Eugenia smoothed the lapels on her smoking jacket. Few women could get away with dressing as she did, crossing over the gender roles at her own pleasure. She was a force of an individual, and an even more so, as a woman who had no time for what feminists were trying to accomplish, because she'd never cared much for what men thought of her, her family, or her decisions. Colleen respected the hell out of her. She wanted her approval, more than any of them, because only in Eugenia's presence did Colleen ever find her own attempts at successful self-awareness lacking.

"All in favor of Luther being our seventh Council member, raise your hand and say 'aye.'"

Pansy was first, throwing her hand in the air with dramatic aplomb, followed by Cassius, and then Pierce. Eugenia shook her head and then raised hers as well, which left only Kitty.

Colleen looked at her younger cousin. "Kitty?"

"I don't have to like it," Kitty replied. "And I don't have to support it. But I'll respect it." She left her palms spread across her notebook.

Colleen sighed inwardly. "Very well." She raised her own hand. "Five for. One against. If Luther agrees to the appointment, then we'll induct him as our seventh member, thereby making us whole once more."

"We'll never be whole without Tante Ophelia," Kitty countered, venom interlacing her words. Her eyes, glassy with tears.

"I thought that, at first," Colleen said, as she tried hard to separate emotion from fact. She'd never seen her aunt cry, or show any emotion beyond passion, and the best way to honor her was to continue with the same strength. "But if she believed we'd all fall apart when she died, well... she wouldn't rest easy at all. She built all this to outlast her, not to crumble at the first sign of a challenge. Ophelia's last words to me were 'now, go and do as you are born to do, so that I can die with the peace of possibility.' I would give her that peace. Would you?"

Kitty tapped her pen and looked down.

"The peace of possibility," Eugenia mused, running her tongue over her bold burgundy lipstick. "How very Ophelia."

"How very," Cassius agreed, hanging his head in solemnity.

"For Ophelia," Pierce said.

"For all of us," Colleen corrected. "Ophelia gave us a gift. She gave us this. Each other. We can honor her by not letting it all be for nothing."

She didn't wait for responses this time. Instead, she called the meeting adjourned and left without joining in the tradition of tea and biscuits. It was past one in the morning, and though her two loves would be asleep when she slipped upstairs, even their slowed breaths were a balm to her tormented soul.

Colleen was happy. For the first time in her life, she understood that happiness wasn't numbers on a grading sheet, or accolades for achievement.

But she feared admitting to anyone that she was well over her head. That she feared being magistrate, returning to college, all of it, would end up affecting her role as wife and mother, in a way that might be irreparable. Her fears, which had been with her throughout her whole life, reminding her what failure would both bring and take, had never spoken louder than when she had something real, tangible, *irreplaceable* to lose.

Noah's soft, warm snuggle as she slipped in beside him was enough to wash away these fears, at least for tonight.

By the time Charles dropped Colin off at home that night, they were both exhausted, both physically and emotionally. They kept their emotions to themselves, letting them live only in the tension cutting the air between them in the car, or the occasional burst of words born of fear and anger. Charles and Colin, two men who loved the same woman, and now, in their own ways, for their own reasons, also hated her.

They'd driven all over New Orleans, visiting anyone at all

Catherine knew even casually. Old friends from college, from high school. Her college roommate. Cousins, and even an old boyfriend. None of them had heard anything at all about Catherine. Most hadn't heard from or talked to her in many years. Colin seemed surprised by this, but Charles wasn't. Charles, who'd paid attention to who Catherine was at her roots and not just at the surface, understood that she'd never had many real friends. She was too fickle, too unmoored, and her childhood instability led her to think of any relationship in her life as transient, to protect herself. It didn't make her erratic, on-again, off-again love of Charles any easier to bear, but it explained things.

Jeannie, Catherine's old roommate, provided the only potential clue, and she'd had the good sense to whisper it to Charles, out of earshot of Colin, as they were leaving.

"Talk to your sister."

"Which one?"

"The nosy one. The busybody. I forget her name."

"Colleen?"

Jeannie snorted. "That's the one."

"What does Colleen have to do with this?"

"Indeed," Jeannie said and closed the door.

Colin asked him what that was about, when Charles got to the car, and he had to make something up about Jeannie asking for a hookup on some cocaine. Colin looked appropriately skeptical but didn't probe. Colin thought he wanted answers, but he didn't, really.

When they stopped for lunch at Camellia Grill, Charles excused himself to make a call at the payphone. He said he was checking in on Nicolas, but the number he dialed, reaching into his little black phonebook to find, was The Gardens.

He didn't give Colleen a chance for small talk when she came to the phone. "I need to know what you have to do with Catherine's disappearance."

Silence for a moment on her end and then, "I heard about Catherine. I'm sorry. What have the police said?"

"Don't play coy with me, Leena. What do you know about it?"

"Why would I know anything about Catherine?"

"That's not a fucking answer."

"Maybe it's not the one you're looking for," she said. "But it's the one you're getting. I don't have time for your strange whims today, Huck. I need to finish feeding Amelia."

The phone went dead in his hand. His cheeks flushed with rage, and he started to fish for more coins, to call her back, but Colin staring at him from across the diner gave him pause. The drawn look of pain painting his face was an ever present reminder that Charles had contributed to this mess. He didn't drive Catherine away—she'd been looking for an escape when she called him that night, months ago. But surely her confused feelings for him played a part in the unhappiness of her marriage, and Colin didn't deserve any of this.

It was easy, sometimes, for Charles to justify his behavior by marking his friend as insufferable, but Colin was the only person he knew who lived by such a strong moral code that he never wavered from what was right. Good or bad, problematic or not, Colin was the definition of a good man. Everything he did, he did because he believed it was the right thing to do. He may lack the imagination for a wife like Catherine, but that was not the same as being undeserving. If anyone in this world deserved happiness, it was Colin Sullivan.

Charles continued their quest to find Catherine after lunch, even though he knew it was pointless. She was gone. She'd left New Orleans, and their reach and connections dwindled the farther the proximity from the city.

"We'll find her," Charles promised weakly, as Colin shifted his weight into the door, to lift himself from the car. His shoulders hung with exhaustion, and Charles found he couldn't look his friend in the face, for fear of what he might see there.

"Thanks for today, Huck," Colin said, without turning for a

proper goodbye. Charles waited until Colin lumbered into the house and closed the door behind him, before pulling away.

"Where did you go, Cat?" Charles wondered aloud, in equal parts curiosity and anger, as he returned to his surrogate wife and only son; as he returned after having spent the day chasing ghosts, once again lured into the trap laid by his first, and maybe only, real love.

I'm not that man anymore, he thought, as he always did whenever she'd managed to pull him back into the web she'd woven for him and him alone.

CHAPTER 3
Science and Nature

Evangeline almost didn't join the study group. The last time she'd joined something, that "astronomy club" for Tulane students, it turned out to be a convenient credit-accruing cover for people more concerned with drugs and partying. That same group then led to some of the worst months of her entire life, and a change in how she saw herself fundamentally. Only with the distance of time could Evangeline see just how soundly what happened to her in that old warehouse had shaped who she was and who she would become.

For instance, she knew she'd never move home to New Orleans, something she'd realized only recently.

But this club was long established at MIT; one that the campus itself endorsed and encouraged, unlike the astronomy club that she'd found through the classifieds in the Times-Picayune. They met on campus only, in a quiet corner room of the library the school reserved for the club, and there was an official process to sign up, which allowed the college to vet any members and confirm they were, in fact, students. Everything about this study group read as SAFE, CLEAN, INVITING. Neon letters optional.

She needed *something*, that much was clear. Having kept to

herself for her first year, she'd been fine living as a relative loner until that loneliness caught up and hit her with gale wind force. It was fine until it wasn't, as her family liked to say.

So far, she loved it.

The MIT Study Crew had several different groups within the main one. Each met at different times, in their private library office. Evangeline chose the overnight crew, which had less membership and attendance than the others, but she wasn't sleeping anyway, so it was better than lying awake and letting her imagination take her to bad places.

The Midnight Marauders, as one of the third-years dubbed them, consisted of three to five students, depending on the night. There was Ian, the Statistics major, who never spoke, choosing instead to communicate through his scratchpad or his own peculiar version of charades. Back in New Orleans, kids would have teased someone like Ian, but here, among the most brilliant minds in science and tech, his otherness wasn't other at all. Janice was a Biochem major who put eleven scoops of sugar in her coffee, which she was always drinking, even well into the early morning hours when they all went back to their dorms and apartments. Whenever she asked Evangeline, a general Chemistry student, for her opinion, she did so at the frequency of a honeybee. Evan was an Engineering major from Canada, who used the chalkboard nonstop, and not gently. He often did his thinking out loud and tried to bring others into it, especially Sven, the other Engineering major in the group, who was from Norway. Sven's English was not fantastic, so they spent most of their exchanges trying to find new ways to communicate his questions.

The last of the group, Cassie, was in the newly-formed Computer Sciences program. She was from a small town in Oregon that had little to no educational funding, and had tested so far above the other students that her principal himself had reached out to different schools to try and help get her placed somewhere worthy of her talents. Unlike all the others in the Midnight Marauders, Cassie was the only undergrad, a second year who kept mostly to herself, but when she did speak, had plenty to say.

Evangeline liked Cassie. The first time she met her wasn't at study group, but passing in the quad. Cassie stopped to break up a colorful fight between some young lovers, standing up to the man, who was at least a foot taller, without fear or hesitation. He smirked at the young woman daring to challenge him, but something in her eyes caused him to back down. Evangeline came upon the scene, Cassie comforting the girl but standing firm in her advice that she should notify someone of the abuse. She even offered to accompany the young woman to the police.

Evangeline didn't stop, or say anything then, but when she met Cassie officially in the study group, she knew immediately they'd be friends. Cassie was the kind of person who was more concerned with what was right than being liked, and that was a trait Evangeline didn't know she needed in a friend until she saw it in Cassandra Collins.

Cassie lived on campus, like many of the undergrads, but her dormitory was on the way to Evangeline's apartment, so they walked together each morning after study group, just before the sun crested over the eastern horizon. Evangeline would wave as Cassie disappeared inside the glass doors, as she continued another four blocks to her own place, which lay at the outer edge of campus.

One night, huddled together under an umbrella as the spring rains assaulted them, Cassie stopped by a covered bulletin board that held announcements and requests for roommates, sales of items, and other various things. Evangeline, freezing cold, told her to come on, but Cassie was firm.

"Look at this, Evangeline," she said, jabbing her finger at a poster larger than any of the other announcements. The top of the black and white printout said MISSING. The face below was their age; a young woman with dark hair, a strong nose, and a beautiful smile. "Darcy Banks, missing since last week. She's a student here. Do you know her?"

Evangeline shook her head.

"Says her boyfriend saw her the night before she went missing. You think he did it?"

"Statistics aren't in his favor," Evangeline replied.

Cassie made a light sound, both humor and hardness. "Scary is all. You know?"

"I grew up in New Orleans," Evangeline said. "Girls went missing all the time, unfortunately." *Some survived but were worse for it.*

"A girl in my small town was assaulted once," Cassie said. Her finger still made its way over the plastic covering the flier, scanning the details. "It was a very big deal. The whole town came to a stop until the case was solved."

"We had very different upbringings."

"We did," Cassie said. "But life is life. It has value, whether you grew up in a town with three thousand, or three million."

Evangeline nodded. This was true, of course, and being hardened to the fact didn't change that this girl, Darcy Banks, mattered. The odds were not good in finding her alive, given the time that had passed since she was last seen, but she was someone's daughter. Someone's friend. Someone. "Look at the bottom. They're asking for volunteers to knock on doors."

"Yeah." Cassie had a faraway look in her eyes, one that made Evangeline want to know where she went.

"We could do that?" She formed it as a question, rather than a solid suggestion, and didn't know why.

"We should do that," Cassie agreed. "In fact, Evangeline Deschanel, I think we *will* do that." She dug into her bag for a pen and wrote the phone number for volunteers on the inside of her palm. "I'll ring this after a couple good hours of the snoozefest calling my name at the end of this path. If you've got anything on your social calendar, move it."

. . .

MAUREEN HAD BEEN TAUGHT THAT SELF-PLEASURE WAS a sin, and so she'd adroitly avoided anything resembling it. It was one of the few teachings of her childhood she followed. She didn't know why she chose this, and nothing else, to adhere to her moral standards. Surely her promiscuity in her teenage years was *more* of a sin, but somehow, to her, it felt less so, perhaps because she knew they were created by God in order to procreate.

This rule of hers was now contributing to some of her unhappiness. Not total unhappiness; she was born anew in the love of her daughter, Olivia, who was a year old now, and Maureen really had adjusted to being the mistress of Blanchard House, even if their St. Charles mansion *was* rather dark and depressing. But her husband's insistence on an abstinent marriage meant that Maureen's own needs, which had always been so loud, screaming at her in their impatience, went unanswered. She knew very well that he practiced no such teetotaling where his own sexual desires were concerned. The rumors she once ignored when she was only his young, beautiful secretary were now permeating her life as his wife, and he'd gone through three, maybe four young women just like her in their short marriage.

Maureen tried not to care about this. She was sensible enough to know this was the way of things between them and had no designs on changing his proclivities. But it put a finer point on her own sexual misery, and if he could satisfy his urges, then why couldn't she?

She worked up the courage to have this conversation with him over their shared dinnertime—the only time, really, that they were ever alone together unless they were attending an event, and that wasn't the same at all. The thirty minutes together, her gazing at him across the longest dining room table in the world, it seemed, waiting for acknowledgement, or even a smile, was her time to get his attention, if she needed it. His mood always dictated how much of it he was willing to offer.

She passed Olivia to the part-time nanny. When the woman

was gone, she straightened her spine and went for it, before she could lose her courage. "Husband."

Edouard flipped the newspaper page without looking at her. "Wife."

"I was hoping we could talk about something."

"That's what we're doing," he said, nose down on his glasses as he read, more than likely, the local news section, which was where he always started. "Talking."

"I was hoping..." Maureen trailed off as one of the kitchen staff entered and placed their plates in front of them. Edouard asked what she was hoping, but she didn't answer until they were alone again. "To talk to you without the newspaper covering your face."

Edouard grunted. He didn't at first heed her request, but after a second, louder grunt, he folded the paper and set it neatly at his left. "I haven't gotten to the baseball scores, so I'd appreciate your expediency."

"I'll try," she said. So many of their conversations happened from behind his newspaper that she didn't quite know what to do with his undivided attention. She started to chew her lip, but remembered he didn't like that, or any habits that went against his quest for fastidiousness in all things. "I don't quite know how to say it."

Edouard sliced through his steak with his knife. He dabbed it in a dark sauce and placed it gently into his mouth, like a jeweler tending to a rare diamond. He chewed, swallowed, and then said, "Expediency, Maureen."

You should be so lucky to have a wife as young and beautiful as me. To have a wife who would do anything to make you happy and dotes on your only daughter.

"I know you have your pet projects on the side." She sucked in and held her breath, with the first of the words out and lying in the space between them.

"Pet projects," he repeated, enunciating each word with careful precision.

"You know what I mean."

He set his fork aside. "I'm not sure that I do."

Maureen sighed. "Your secretaries, Edouard. I know I wasn't the first, and I didn't expect to be the last."

Edouard tensed. He didn't immediately respond.

"I'm *fine* with it," she stressed. "Really, I am. You won't hear a word about it from me."

"And yet, here you are, with words about it."

"Not about that," she said, shaking her head. She needed to get to the point before he got cross with her, a state in which he was already halfway there. "I want you to be happy. To be *satisfied.* As your wife, this is my utmost concern in all the world, even if it's not me you choose to satisfy yourself with."

Edouard's face twitched. Another pointed silence followed as one of the kitchen staff came to refill their wine glasses.

"But, as you have needs, well, so do I," Maureen said, proud of herself for coming to the point. She'd said it. Women were not supposed to have such needs, according to polite society, but, well, Maureen knew who she was and there was no use denying it. "And I'm not asking for much, but I do need something."

Edouard's cheeks blossomed with pink. She couldn't read his expression, to decipher whether he was embarrassed at her choice of conversation, or angry at her impudence. "I see."

"I know what our marriage is. What we agreed to. Other than that one time, I've... well, I've respected that. I've adjusted my expectations, and my needs, accordingly. I've been a wonderful mother to our daughter, I take care of the household—"

"Maureen—"

"And I wouldn't ask if it weren't so... well, unfair, that you can carry on as you please, while I'm left going to bed each night frustrated." Maureen held her breath; she'd gone too far, she was sure of it.

"If you're expecting me to shame you for having needs," Edouard said slowly, "you're mistaken. I don't wish to discuss this in any great detail, please understand, but as a man who has...

peculiar needs of his own, I'm in no place to judge those of others."

"Twice a week, it's all I ask," Maureen blurted. "You don't need to pretend to be into it. I just need... I need the act, Edouard. I need to feel..." She trailed off.

He shook his head. "We may be on two different tracks here. What I've told you, about our own conjugal relationship, still stands. I'll come to your bed if and when you want another child, and only then."

Maureen's lip quavered. She willed it to be still, to act like an adult. "I don't understand."

Edouard checked his watch. She let her eyes travel to the clock above his head and noted he had only fifteen minutes left in his allotted time for dinner before his persnickety routine would require him to transition to time in his study. "Our meals are getting cold. I'm giving you permission to do what you need to in order to see your needs are met." He picked up his fork. "With someone else."

"You're... what?"

He sighed in impatience. "An affair, Maureen. An affair with someone of your choosing. I don't care to know about it, and if I find out, I'll be exceptionally displeased at your lack of discretion. And that *is* all I ask of you. Discretion. Meet with this... this whoever he'll be, somewhere our own people don't go. Out of town, even. I don't care. I don't want the details." He began to tear neatly into his steak again.

"You want me to have an affair?" she repeated, in shock.

"I don't *want* you to do anything," Edouard replied, when he was done chewing. "But what I do want is for this to not come up again between us, and it seems as if it will unless you find an outlet for your own needs. I'm giving you one, on the condition we don't speak of this again, and no one in our social circles ever finds out."

"An affair," she said again, musing. This was not at all what she had in mind, but it was... it was...

It was better.

Edouard was not a handsome man. He was over twice her age, with nothing, other than his money and success, going for him. She'd come looking for a consolation prize, and he'd given her the whole trophy.

Any man she wanted.

And why limit herself to one?

Maureen could have many men. Handsome men. *Passionate* men.

The endlessness of these delicious possibilities replaced what remained of her appetite.

Edouard took her silence as assent apparently, as he disappeared again behind his newspaper.

NOAH SAT DOWN ACROSS FROM HIM, HIS FACE PAINTED with a level of patience he must have mustered up on the entire drive over. Charles knew his brother-in-law didn't like him. His own memory was hazy where his high school days were concerned, but he vaguely recalled giving Noah Jameson a hard time about *something*. That didn't make Noah unique. That he'd married Charles' sister, however, did.

"I'm here," Noah said, pleasantly enough. "You wanted to talk?"

"Yeah, yeah," Charles said, folding and refolding his arms. He felt antsy, the way he used to when he'd go a couple days without blow. "Thanks. I do want to talk."

"If it's about Colleen—"

"It's not," Charles said quickly. "Not *exactly.*"

"What does that mean? Not exactly?"

"It's not about Colleen, but it's about what she might know."

"Sorry, I'm really not following, Charles."

"When are you going back to Scotland?"

"What?"

"I didn't mean to confuse you with a simple question."

"I'm confused, all right," Noah muttered. "I don't know why we're here, and why I couldn't bring Colleen."

"Because Colleen is lying to me," Charles said. "I'm hoping you have better sense."

Noah peeled back. "Look, I'm not an easy target anymore. You don't scare me."

Noah was going to leave if Charles didn't rein this in. "I'm sorry, brother. Nicolas still isn't sleeping much, and so neither am I." He rubbed his face. "I think Colleen knows where Catherine went, and if she knows, you probably do, too."

"Catherine?"

He was going to make him say it. Make him play the game. "Sullivan?"

"What's it to you where your friend's wife is?" Noah said. The hint of cheekiness in his voice revealed that he knew *exactly* what it was to Charles.

Charles wouldn't give him the satisfaction, though. "What it is to me is that my best friend is in pain because his wife and son have fallen off the face of the earth."

Noah held up his hands. "I don't know anything about it. Sorry."

"Colleen does," Charles pressed.

"Colleen and Catherine are not friends, as far as I know."

"Did I say they were?"

"Seems to me you're grasping at straws," Noah said. He leaned forward. "Look, I know Colin Sullivan. He's a good guy. If I hear anything, I'll tell him. But you're barking up the wrong tree."

He had half a mind to call Augustus. Augustus would make this Irish mick asshole spill his guts about this and every other sin he'd ever committed.

But Augustus deserved a break from fixing everyone else's problems. According to Elizabeth, he was barely holding his own life together.

"Am I?"

Noah's laugh was far from amused. "Why would Colleen know anything about where Colin's wife is?"

"You tell me."

Noah threw out his hands. "We done?"

"For now."

Noah stood, reaching into his wallet for some cash. He threw a five on the table. "Don't bother Colleen about this again. She's got enough to deal with, and I won't have anyone adding to her stress." He frowned and then added, "Please."

Charles watched Noah leave, more than ever convinced that his sister and brother-in-law knew a lot more than they were letting on.

CHAPTER 4
Somebody to Love

The wedding of Patrick Sullivan to his longtime love, Isabella Livingston, was held at Destrehan plantation, down St. Charles Parish. Charles remarked offhand that he had a better plantation to offer them and wouldn't even have charged a cent, but Destrehan was only forty minutes from the city, where Ophélie was well over an hour.

Charles nodded at the explanation, satisfied, but Augustus knew better. Patrick, like every other Sullivan, it seemed, *except* Colin, knew Charles' role in the troubled marriage between Colin and Catherine, and wasn't about to receive a handout from a homewrecker.

The weather was unseasonably warm, even for the subtropical South, so Augustus purchased extra sun protection for Anasofiya's pram, as well as a mosquito net to drape over the open area. She was too young for him to know whether or not she'd have any kind of allergic reaction to bites, and although the last yellow fever case was in 1905, one could never be too careful. There were also bees to consider.

Elizabeth stuck to his side as if glued there, and Connor followed suit, flanking his other side. Every time he tried to tell her this wasn't necessary, she fired back with a range of comebacks he lacked the emotional fortitude to challenge. She wasn't hurting anything, he supposed. She'd started to understand his need for boundaries, and no longer pushed so hard against them.

After the first sad, sympathetic glance from a wedding-goer, Augustus knew coming to this wedding was a bad idea. He'd had his reservations from the moment the invitation arrived. Bringing Ana out of the house, making her ride in a car for so long, had its own risks, but well-meaning friends and family would undoubtedly try to force Augustus into unwelcome conversation and false platitudes surrounding the fate of his late wife. He'd already promised himself the topic was off-limits. Not only with others, but himself.

Where Ana was concerned, she would know only that Ekatherina had never wanted anything more in her life than a daughter, and was, of course, watching over her from heaven.

"That kid is so stinkin' cute," Connor remarked as Rory and Carolina both lifted toddler Clancy with their hands, laughing as he smiled and kicked at the air. "I've missed him."

Augustus should go talk to them. To Carolina, especially, who still asked after him, from time to time.

Instead, he navigated the baby carriage in another direction.

"Not gonna say hi?" Elizabeth asked, keeping up. He shot her a sidelong glance. She already knew the answer.

"Let's go find seats."

"No one else is finding seats," Elizabeth challenged.

"Are we everyone else, Elizabeth?"

"No, *Dad,*" she huffed, but went on ahead to see about finding their spots.

"I never met your father, but the way Lizzy describes him, you two—"

Augustus pointed his gaze at Connor. "She didn't mean it as a compliment."

"Oh."

Elizabeth jogged back up in her light blue dress, navigating the damp grass in satin heels. Without asking, she lifted Ana into her arms and commanded Augustus to go park the stroller by the tree. Before he could protest, she was off, Connor looking helplessly between them before following.

Irish Colleen saddled up beside him. "The decorations are beautiful."

"Yeah."

"Must be nice for you to be out of the house? With Ana?"

"I'll feel better when she's safe at home."

"Now, Augustus," Irish Colleen said, tone harkening back to the one used when attempting to convey the important life lessons of their childhood, "children need to be outdoors."

"She's not a child. She's a baby."

"She'll be pale-faced and mealy-mouthed if you have your way."

"I don't even know what that means."

"Like those kids whose parents hide them in attics, away from the world."

"No one does that, Mama. You're making that up."

"Am I?"

Augustus couldn't argue with his mother's logic, which, in her mind, was irrefutable. She dealt in old wives' tales and superstitions, never one to let facts get in the way of a story that might scare the insolent children into better behavior.

"Babies are far more resilient than you think," she said, taking his arm. "If you knew how many times I'd dropped you on your head..."

"Mama!"

Irish Colleen smiled from the side of her mouth. She was actually making a *joke.* There was a first for everything. "Not really, but I did drop you once. I dropped all of you at some point. I also let you eat dirt and crawl around on dusty floors from time to time. You survived in spite of my criminal neglect."

"I don't believe you."

She laughed. "It's true!"

Augustus shook his head. "No way. Your floors were *never* dusty."

Elizabeth stood on a chair and waved both arms over the crowd of wedding-goers making their way forward.

"Those chairs are *white*," Maureen chided, appearing at Augustus' right side, holding Olivia's hand as the little one toddled at her side. Her husband wasn't with her.

"Only Lizzy," Irish Colleen muttered, still smiling as she let Augustus lead them to their seats.

UNLIKE THIS TIME THE PRIOR YEAR, WHERE COLLEEN feared the moment she would reveal to everyone she loved that she was *in* love and getting married, she was excited to introduce Noah to her circle of friends and family at the Sullivan-Livingston wedding. She beamed as she told and retold the story of how they met, where they fell in love. They exchanged glances when recalling how foolish love could be, and how wrong they were to ever think they could live without one another. She blushed as she held out her hand for others to admire Noah's creative choice to overlay gold to the withering heather he'd used to declare his intentions.

All the women gushed over her stories. Chelsea elbowed Mason and lifted her brows in the most romantic parts, and Mason pretended not to take her meaning. Carolina and Isabella exchanged looks—they'd both married Sullivans, they knew the drill. Pansy and Kitty both remarked that they didn't believe a word, through their jealous eyes and smiles that showed they were, in fact, happy for Colleen. They all promised to come visit with Amelia, who was spending the day with Kellan Jameson so Colleen and Noah could have a few hours with their friends.

It felt good, for once, to be the woman in the room with something to share other than her ambitions.

But what she desperately wanted was time alone with Rory

and Carolina. She'd have to be very careful how she went about getting it, after Charles' shakedown of Noah.

She found her chance at the reception. Charles had a few drinks in him and had occupied himself with several of the bridesmaids, taking his turns dancing with them and likely making plans with at least one of them for later.

Colleen slipped her hand through Noah's and nodded toward the hall, where Rory and Carolina beckoned. They followed their friends into a parlor, where Rory closed and locked the double doors behind them.

"Where's Clancy?" Noah asked.

Carolina answered. "With Colin."

"Catherine," Colleen said with a long exhale, not wasting time.

"She's great," Carolina replied. She looked healthy, radiant in her carnation gown. Colleen couldn't help remembering Carolina of only two years ago, drained of color and health, on death's doorstep. "Under the circumstances."

"Ready to pop, if you ask me," Rory added, and Carolina gave him a look that said, *no one asked you.*

"Has Charles called you guys?" Noah asked.

Colleen tried not to look at him; he was even more handsome than usual in his tuxedo and cummerbund. His bowtie sent her heart surging.

Rory and Carolina exchanged looks.

"No, why?" Rory asked. "He doesn't know, does he? Tell me he doesn't know!"

"No, no," Colleen said quickly. She kept glancing back at the door, as if it might open, despite being locked. Charles appeared, red-faced and furious, in her imagination. "He doesn't *know* anything. But someone told him I might know something."

"Who?" Carolina asked.

"We don't know," Colleen said. "And it's not a good idea for us to go asking around, under the circumstances. He's been calling me, and even tricked Noah into meeting him so he could give him the third degree, too."

Rory lifted his arms over his head. His groomsman jacket flapped at his sides. "This is *not* good. If Charles finds out what's going on, this is over. The whole thing is off. Colin would kill me if he ever—"

Carolina stepped in front of him and seized his arms. "Rory, stop. Charles won't find out, because only the four of us know. Remember?"

"Did you hear what they said?"

"I did, did you?" Carolina pulled his arms to his sides again. "They said Charles thinks he knows something. But unless he hears what's really going on, from one of us, he *knows* nothing. Right?"

"I don't know... this isn't good."

"It's fine," Noah said. "He won't hear it from us, or you, so we have nothing to worry about. Colleen and I can handle Charles and his chest puffing. Just worry about Catherine, and the little girl she needs to bring safely into this world."

Rory calmed with Carolina's touch. "Okay, but you'll tell us if you think he's got the score."

"We will," Colleen assured him, "but he won't. If he hasn't contacted you already, then he never will."

"It will all be over soon," Carolina added, for her husband's sake. "Once Robyn is born, we will help Catherine recover and then send her home."

"You'll have to tell Colin she was with you, you know," Noah said. "After the fact."

Rory blinked. Color drained from his face. "Colin would *never* forgive that."

"Wrong," Colleen said. "He'll be sore that you kept it from him, but knowing his wife was safe with his brother is the best comfort we can give him after this long absence. You know that. If she wasn't with you, then where was she? And with whom? Colin will believe you, and it will put his mind at ease. He deserves that, and if he thinks she was at some undisclosed place, he'll never have peace about it, Rory. Never."

"Colleen is right," Carolina said. "We have to tell him, and we just say we were respecting Catherine's right to privacy."

"He'll never forgive me," Rory said again.

"It's not about you, though, is it?" Noah answered. "You already have to come up with an excuse for not telling anyone Carolina was expecting. Combine them into one."

"I don't follow."

"Your secrecy around Carolina's 'pregnancy,' is about your worry for her," Noah went on. He paced in front of the fireplace. Colleen fell in love with him over and over as she watched him; listened to him take control. "When Catherine asked for help, you decided Catherine could help you, too, by staying with Carolina and seeing her through her difficult time. If Carolina has no difficult time, you have no reason for keeping this news to yourself."

Rory nodded as he listened. "You think like a lawyer, Noah."

Noah winced. "I'll leave that to you."

"We always knew there would be parts of this plan no one else could ever know," Colleen jumped in. "Colin will understand your love of your wife, because of his love for his own."

Noah winked at her from across the parlor, one arm draped over the mantle of the fireplace, suit jacket hanging open. She couldn't wait to get him back to The Gardens.

"I pray you're right," Rory said.

"They are right," Carolina said, slipping her hands into his pockets as she leaned in for a kiss. "And soon, we'll have a beautiful daughter, and not even Colin, in his infinite anger and hurt and fear, could ever begrudge us that."

"Convince Catherine to call Colin to check in," Noah said. "So he knows she's okay, and Oz is okay. Help her with a believable story, but whatever she says can't bring Colin to your doorstep. She calls home, he calls off the dogs. He calls off *Charles.* You do that, and we can all breathe until Robyn is born."

"Robyn," Colleen said, smiling. "What a beautiful name."

Carolina blushed. "Robyn Elizabeth. We plan to call her Ari, for short."

Rory seemed to remember what mattered most about all of this, as he slipped his arms around his wife's waist and, leaning close to her, said, "We can't wait to meet her."

Chelsea slipped the flask from the inside of her left cowboy boot. When Maureen flashed her a scandalized expression, Chelsea shrugged and took a long sip off the metal flagon before replacing it.

"I'm breastfeeding," Maureen felt compelled to say, to explain away what Chelsea evidently thought was her total squaredom.

"Your loss," Chelsea replied. She waved at her husband, Mason, a gesture to say to go find his own fun for a bit. She dug in her dress for a pack of cigarettes, frowned at Maureen as she lit one, and tucked them away again. "Where is your little crotch monkey, anyway?"

"Chelsea!"

"Well?"

"*Olivia's* with my mother."

"I hope my mom isn't too tired from minding my brothers' children when Mason and I finally squirt out some little ones."

"Vulgar."

Chelsea blew out her smoke. "You love it."

"Not really, not anymore. When you're a mother, you'll understand."

"Oh?" Chelsea laughed. "Does becoming a mother cause one to lose their sense of humor?"

"No, but you might see certain things as not entirely ladylike. You start thinking of the impression you're leaving on the young women you're raising."

Chelsea took a long drag. "I don't intend to have girls, Maureen. I know better." She leveled a meaningful look on

Maureen, then held up her hand, pretending it was a mirror. This made Maureen laugh.

"I don't want Livvy to end up like her Mama," Maureen confessed. Chelsea was always both her best and worst confidante. Best, because she gave direct, no-nonsense advice and genuinely loved Maureen. Worst, because any time she shared something not-so-great about herself, it shattered the princess-like image Maureen wanted to convey to the world, and *especially* girls like Chelsea. "I want better for her."

"All parents want a better life for their kids. That's the whole point of procreating."

"Is it?"

"What else could there be?"

"Love? Nurturing?"

"Sure," Chelsea replied. She stubbed her cigarette under her boot. "But, really, Maureen, people who actually give a shit about being good parents, and have worries like yours, aren't the ones fucking their kids up for life."

"How do you figure?"

"Bad parents think they're amazing parents and don't have self-awareness or introspection to assess themselves any different than their delusions tell them to. Good parents stress constantly about being bad parents, so much so that their kids probably *wish* they were bad parents so they could go have a sleepover from time to time, or kiss a boy."

Maureen played with the knit on her shawl. "I see. You're an expert, then."

Chelsea knelt to draw another sip from her boot flask. When she stood, she asked, "Why are you so concerned, anyway? You'd stop the world for Livvy. You're a great mom."

"Thank you," Maureen said, flushing. "It's not me, so much, that I'm worried about."

Chelsea slipped her arm through Maureen's, hooking elbows, and aimed her toward a copse of trees. "Go on."

"I don't know if I should. Mama always taught us you should keep your laundry in your own hamper."

"Irish Colleen has a saying for everything, but that doesn't mean half of what she says makes any damn sense."

Maureen chuckled. She'd often thought the same thing about her long-suffering, superstitious mother. "It's only... well, it's my husband."

"Ebenezer Scrooge."

"Chelsea!"

"Am I wrong?"

"Are you going to listen, or just run your mouth and say mean things?"

Chelsea threw her free hand up.

"Anyway," Maureen went on. "He and I aren't... well, we aren't close, if you know where I'm going with this."

"You don't fuck?"

"Chel*sea*!"

"Fine, fine. He's not exercising his God-given right for conjugal visitation with his legal wife."

Maureen rolled her eyes. "His right to me isn't God-given, thank you, but no, he's not exercising his... whatever you just said. I don't want to get into it, but you'll remember some of what I told you back when I was his secretary."

"Let's just say if I was a writer, that story would be ingrained in Americana by now." Chelsea navigated them through the maze of cypress, nudging Maureen when they nearly tripped over a knobby kneed root. "I get your point about Edouard. But what does that have to do with Olivia?"

"Only that..." Maureen had trouble saying the words. "I grew up mostly without a father, and look how I turned out."

"The woman walking next to me is a dedicated mother who runs her own household, and she's not even twenty. What am I missing?"

"You know what I mean."

"Daddy issues," Chelsea said, nodding. "But you sell yourself short, Maureen. You're assuming you're not giving Olivia enough as her mother, which isn't true. Forgive me for saying this, but you're way more nurturing than Irish Colleen. It's a fact."

Maureen took no offense to the statement, because she, too, recognized her mother's greatest accomplishments as their parent were keeping them fed and alive. "It's more than Olivia. It's me."

"Women have needs," Chelsea agreed. "Men aren't the only ones. They like us to worship at the altar of dick, and then when we want some, too, they're confused? Sorry, but that's bullshit."

"I told him as much recently... but not in those words." Maureen wrinkled her nose. "I definitely didn't refer to the altar of dick."

"Should've. Sometimes they like it when we talk like them."

Maureen shook her head. "No, not Edouard. He's not like any man I've ever known."

"So what did he say? About your needs?"

"He told me to get a lover."

Chelsea stopped abruptly in the soft mossy grass. She doubled over, laughing. "I thought you lost your sense of humor when you pissed out a daughter."

"I'm not being funny! He'd rather his wife take a damn lover than touch her himself!"

Chelsea righted herself. Wiped her eyes, which was clearly for dramatic effect because they weren't damp. "Wow. And you said thank you, right?"

Maureen chewed on her bottom lip. "Something like that."

"Maureen." Chelsea grabbed both her arms. "Don't you understand? This is like... winning the Nobel Prize. Being an Olympian. Winning the lottery!"

"It's really like none of those thin—"

"It's as if a genie swooped down and offered you his greatest wish!"

"No, it's not a bad thing," Maureen agreed. "But where on earth am I going to find a lover? One who is handsome, discreet, available?"

"Sweetie. You've fucked half of New Orleans, and you're afraid there's not one man who will check those boxes?"

"I have *not* fucked half of New Orleans."

Chelsea looked dubious. "I know we're pretending you were a little 4-H queen who showed lambs instead of the wolf who stole the virginity of every last one of them, but *Maureen. Come on.* You know there's hundreds of men who fit that description. And you have an in with a whole firm of lawyers who can ensure his discretion, should he decide to get mouthy in a bar or something."

"I guess."

Chelsea dropped her hands as her eyes filled with the start of an idea. "Maureen." She socked Maureen in the arm. "I have just the guy for you!"

"Ow," Maureen whined, rubbing her triceps. "Who?"

"He comes into Mason's bar all the time."

"Mason's bar... you mean the one in the Irish Channel? You can't be serious. I don't want herpes!"

Chelsea pretended to wipe something from Maureen's nose. "Careful. Your privilege is showing. For your information, there are plenty of amazing, hard-working men who come into Landry's. But this guy isn't one of them."

"Huh?"

"His name is Soren. He's a LaViolette, and I'm sure you know *that* name."

"Rich, snobby assholes. Sure."

"Hi, pot, meet kettle."

Maureen rolled her eyes once more. "Anyway?"

"Soren LaViolette isn't as important as some of his more prominent relatives. He's not close enough to the line of descent for them to care what he does, so this fella is a poet. A *poet*, Maureen. Wears his hair shaggy, like Jim Morrison, drinks only absinthe, which we now have to stock just for him, and spends hours tapping his pen against his temple as he thinks up *really deep and important words.*"

"Are you sure he isn't interested in men?"

"He spends more time watching women walk back and forth across the bar than he does writing the next Great American Poem, so yeah, I'm sure."

"Soren," Maureen said. It was an unusual name, but intriguing, in a way, inviting her to learn more. She couldn't recite a single poem from memory, but a man who was concerned with creating passion on the page would surely be interested in creating it between the sheets. And Chelsea might believe he was an "unimportant" LaViolette, but, much like being a Deschanel, or a Fontenot, or a Broussard, anyone bearing that name had a responsibility to uphold the reputation. Even a Guidry. If there was anyone who'd be as concerned as Maureen with maintaining discretion, it would be someone in the same socio-economic circle.

"Soren," Chelsea repeated. "But you can call him Hercules if you want. He'd probably like that shit."

"Okay." Maureen nodded. "Now what?"

"I'll arrange a meeting. You update your diaphragm."

Augustus' chest hurt from holding his breath so much, and for so long. Elizabeth said nothing when he edged his way toward the exit, where the cars were parked. She spoke only through glances on the drive back to New Orleans, casting peripheral looks every few minutes, as if she had something she wanted to say, but was holding back.

Connor was quiet in the back seat. He seemed to take his cues from Elizabeth, which could be good or bad. Great when Elizabeth was in an understanding mood, not so much when she was laying into Augustus.

He didn't wait for them to follow him into the house before he headed upstairs, Ana sleeping on his shoulder. She needed a nap, and so did he. The few hours spent outside the house, outside the city, exhausted them both.

Augustus closed and locked his bedroom door. One look of

judgment from Elizabeth would be enough to send him clear over the edge.

When Ana was nestled into an arrangement of blankets on his bed, he crawled in beside her. He never tired of looking at her; of seeing the spirit of his ancestors under her soft, sleeping face. She was ethereal; not quite real, which only made his fears of losing her that much more acute. She had the delicate bones of her mother, but did she also possess the delicate spirit? When would he know? Would he be too late?

"Daddy loves you," he whispered. She squinted her face, tiny hands balled into fists, as she adjusted in her sleep. Where did she go when she slept? He'd do anything to go there with her.

Only with Ana did he feel alive anymore.

Only with Ana did he fear dying.

But neither of those sensations were greater than his soul-deep, absolute belief that he would somehow fail her, and that failure would be irreversible.

She squeezed his index finger with her fist. "I'm here," he promised, words that meant so much more.

Anasofiya's little mouth puckered as she relaxed back into dreamland. He loved her more in the span of the half-second gesture than he'd ever loved anyone else, across the space of his life.

Augustus pressed his face into his pillow as the tears flowed. The scream trapped in him since the death of his wife disappeared into the soft cotton.

CHAPTER 5

More Than a Feeling

If one of Augustus' employees had asked to bring their infant child to work, he would've ordered them to find the appropriate childcare. There was a time and place for children. The workplace was neither.

He'd been skirting the edge of his own decision for months. Although he'd returned to work, he worked lean hours, so much so that he felt out of touch with the current events and the growth projections *he'd* set in motion. He could no longer speak confidently about anything happening at Deschanel Media Group, and while a part of him was okay with this, content to disappear into his old home with his daughter until he had a plan to protect her from the world, DMG was *also* his child, in a way. He'd created it from nothing, and, layer by layer, turned it into a successful venture that had prospective employees and investors chomping at the bit to get in on the hottest new act in town.

Bringing Anasofiya to work with him was the only way to both care for her and his business, and if anyone dared point out the hypocrisy of the boss making his own rules, they'd see a new side of Augustus Deschanel.

But no one did.

The women in the office took turns admiring Anasofiya's

shock of red hair and crimson lips, while the men told him they were glad to have him back, and glad to see him find a way to balance his life priorities. If anyone was thinking that Augustus was out of order bringing his baby to work, they neither said it, nor conveyed it in another way. Both his secretaries even offered to watch Ana while Augustus slipped into meetings throughout the day. He was hesitant to do this, but both had children of their own, and this wasn't the battle worth fighting.

In the morning, both Augustus' head of finance, as well as his marketing director, came into his office to brief him. They glanced at the baby in the bassinet, but Ana wasn't a distraction, only a change to the scenery. By afternoon, when people stopped treating him like a new father and more like the head of the company he'd created, Augustus started to relax. Day one could've been a disaster, but instead, it was validation.

He *could* do this. Run a business and raise a daughter.

More importantly, he didn't need anyone's help.

EVANGELINE ANXIOUSLY WATCHED THE CLOCK. THE Midnight Marauders would break soon, and when they did, she'd have to walk across the dark campus, in the middle of what police were calling Terror in the Tech. Seven students missing, all young women. But now four of their bodies had been found. All strangled with some sort of ligature, but not before they were brutally and violently raped.

Including the smiling Darcy Banks, whose face Evangeline greeted every morning and evening, pinned to her apartment fridge.

Police had imposed a curfew for anyone out alone after nine in the evening. For women, they stressed that, even in groups, the risk was too great. All seven of the missing girls were college students. Two from Harvard, one from Boston College, and the remaining four, from MIT.

But Evangeline needed the Midnight Marauders. It was the

closest thing she had to a friend group, and the presence of others with like minds, who expected nothing more than what she could offer, was her tether to sanity. Increased campus patrols surely improved the safety *on* campus, but most of the students had been taken near the campus boundary, not within it. The route to her apartment, once she crossed that boundary, wasn't well lit, a fact that had never occurred to her, or concerned her, until now.

"They say he's handsome," Janice said, breaking the silence.

"Who says?" Evangeline said, resisting the urge to roll her eyes straight to the ceiling. "The missing girls? Or the dead ones?"

"Evie," Cassie cautioned, but she, too, was annoyed.

"He's probably a student," Janice went on. "You know, like one of those losers who were bullied by the pretty girls." She waved her pencil in the air. "*Or* he's an old, ugly fogey who fantasizes about what he can't have." She nodded to herself. "Yeah, that's probably more like it."

"The police haven't released a thing about him, so anything you think you know is just speculation," Cassie chided. "And we're all scientists. We know the danger of speculation."

"I'm not trying to do a citizen's arrest on every loser in town or anything. Sheesh."

"Are you ladies taking a taxi?" Sven asked. Except that wasn't exactly what he said, just the way her brain interpreted his heavy accent.

"They shut them down around campus," Cassie said, scooping her textbook and notes into her bookbag. "After nine."

"Seems counterintuitive to me," Evan offered. "Cautioning women to avoid walking at night, and then removing their means of safe transport."

"He could be transporting his victims by car," Cassie said.

"Maybe they think it will keep us indoors," Janice quipped. "Fat chance. I'm not scared."

You should be, Ian scribbled on the chalkboard, the only words he'd offered all night.

Janice scoffed. "He's only taking the pretty girls."

Evangeline wanted to tell Janice not to sell herself short, but it was true, Janice didn't fit the profile, which the newspaper said was *between the ages of eighteen and twenty-four, physically fit, lean body type, and good-looking according to traditional societal standards.* Janice carried an extra fifty pounds on her—weight that might save her life, in this case. Her face full of acne was additional armor.

"We will walk you," Sven said. "Yes, Evan?"

Evan didn't look at all like he had an interest in walking three girls back to their living quarters, but he agreed, managing to hide at least some of his reluctance. He was probably wishing he hadn't opened his mouth at all.

Evangeline had no time for chivalry, especially the contrived kind, but she did have time for surviving, and if it meant feeling Evan's poorly guarded frustration with having been volunteered until she was safe inside her apartment, she would take it.

She didn't sleep that night. Visions of Serendipity's silky voice, ordering the boys with her to exact their payment from Evangeline, permeated every whip of the wind outside, and every creak from the old apartment. She begged her mind not to take the memory further; she couldn't relive her helplessness, or her inaction. Her just *lying there and taking it*, as if she wanted it, as if she had no tools of her own with which to defend herself. Only later she'd remember her telepathy was a tool, maybe not the best, but one which could be used to confuse and confound; to buy time. Her healing, too, in the right circumstance.

But she hadn't defended herself. She hadn't fought at all, only lay there, wishing there were a place her mind could go to pretend it wasn't happening. Not a day since passed where something in her life didn't remind her of that day, of her failures, her losses.

Nothing, though, brought it to the forefront like the events taking place in Cambridge, Massachusetts.

She should call someone. There was no reason she had to suffer these fears alone. Colleen. Cassie. Both would be there for her, if she needed them.

Evangeline imagined herself making these calls, but she was paralyzed, chained to the bed by her past, by her fears, and by the resurgence of both more swiftly than she was prepared to fight.

Elizabeth tried to skip graduation. She didn't need the crowds, the speeches, the ugly robes, any of it to take her piece of paper and file it away until needed. She disliked the attention; the pride in her mother's eyes, in Colleen's, hell, even in Augustus', made her feel like a trophy on display. It eclipsed any real accomplishment and replaced it with extreme discomfort.

But, she reminded herself, she *did* accomplish something. After thirteen years of school, she never had to return to one ever again. Whatever she lost by not attending college was gained through the peace of mind of knowing she'd never ever be forced to endure the pain and suffering of the masses ever again.

Connor, on the other hand, positively glowed under the shower of adorations from more Sullivans than Elizabeth knew existed—and she'd always thought of them as a massive clan. Even his mother was well enough to attend the austere event, though she clung to her husband's for support.

Connor's cheeks were a perpetual shade of pink as he took the compliments poorly, but eagerly, and explained no less than a hundred times what his plans were. *Tulane. Then, I'll join the firm if they'll have me.* He said the last part as a joke, but there was nothing funny to a Sullivan about being an attorney. Even the ones who did have a sense of humor had no room for anyone who didn't take their family tradition with the highest degree of solemnity.

Connor Sullivan could fail the bar exam a hundred times, and there'd still be a place for him on the esteemed emerald carpets of Sullivan & Associates.

He took breaks from his swarm of family admirers to check on Elizabeth, which she appreciated, and also wished wasn't necessary. She didn't want to need him this much, but if there was one lesson a seer learned in life it was that it didn't matter what the hell you wanted.

"You did well, Lizzy," Augustus said. It was one of the only times she'd seen him without Ana attached, and she wondered who he trusted to take her, even temporarily.

"Thanks."

"I know it wasn't easy."

"Nope."

He squeezed her arm. "I'm proud of you. Dad would be proud."

"Yeah?" She adjusted the uncomfortable new bra Mama bought her for the occasion. *Since when does graduation require a new bra, Mother?* "I don't even remember him."

"You don't?" Augustus, like her other siblings when the topic came up, seemed to realize this for the first time. They all remembered August, even Maureen. They'd all been old enough to make memories with a father they now revered, like he'd been canonized by virtue of his early death. But Elizabeth was only two when he died, and while there were flashes—being held, lying in a bright room listening to the sound of a man's voice—these were not memories. They were not a relationship, which they all got to experience. All except Elizabeth. "He adored you. You were his baby. I think he knew you were the last."

"I was two. Remember?"

Augustus didn't say anything, instead pondering this phenomenon she'd lived with her entire life, in the shadow of a system of memories she wasn't a part of.

She'd lost track of Connor somewhere along the way. She scanned the crowd for him when Colleen hugged her from behind. "Sweet Lizzy. You did it!"

"I did it," Elizabeth repeated. Where was Connor?

"Charles has been looking for you. Did he find you?"

"Yeah. Twice," she said distantly, growing more anxious by the second. "Hey, you seen Connor?"

Colleen frowned. "Last I saw, he was at the punch bowl with Patrick and Jerome. Hey, you okay?"

"Peachy."

"Lizzy." Colleen stepped in front of her. "It's done. You can do whatever you want now."

"Unless it's something you and Mama disapprove of, you mean."

Colleen's budding smile faded. "I already know you don't want to go to college and that's fine. It's your choice, and you're smart enough to make the big choices as much as the small ones."

Elizabeth was so surprised by this she forgot about Connor for a second. "You mean that?"

Colleen kissed her forehead. "Yes, I mean it. I'm proud of you for pushing past everything that held you back and making it to today. I'll be happy if you're happy." She pulled back, and her eyes caught something. "Hey, there's Connor. He's coming... with Mama in tow."

Elizabeth rolled her eyes. "Great. Another lecture about college incoming."

"I... don't think so," Colleen said, without elaborating. "Turn around."

Elizabeth pushed out a heavy sigh and turned. She started to draw in a new one, but the gathered crowd gave her pause.

Her entire family, and half of his, had come to a quiet stop just behind Connor. He'd shed his graduation gown for a suit, and, come to think of it, he was probably wearing the suit underneath all along. She'd been so preoccupied with her own discomfort she'd paid him almost no attention at all.

When he went to his knees, Elizabeth rushed to help him up, thinking he'd gotten a cramp like he sometimes did after physical exercise, but this was no cramp, and the kneeling was no accident.

Elizabeth's pulse surged to the moon. All the blood in her body rushed right into her cheeks.

"Elizabeth Jeanne." Connor's face was as red as hers, and twice as sweaty. What was he doing? Here? Now?

"That's my name," she said, trying not to look at the anxiously shifting crowd, who seemed to know a lot more about what was happening than she did.

Connor's hands were slick, and he tried three times to retrieve something from his pocket, before cursing, rubbing them on his pants, and trying again. She wanted to tell him not to do it, that they could talk about this later, but it was happening, and if he was determined it should happen here, then she couldn't change that.

How had she never seen a vision of this day?

Because it's your own future, silly.

"We don't have to do it today, or tomorrow, or any day, until we want to, which could be tomorrow, I guess, but..." Connor shook his head. "I'm really fumbling this."

"You're fine," she said, but the catch in her voice pushed out the words as a whisper.

"I can't live without you. I love you that much. I guess I've always loved you, before you even knew who I was," Connor went on, his own voice cracking. "And then I loved you more when I knew who you were. Who you were *really*."

"We know how this ends," Elizabeth said, so low she hoped no one else around them could pick up the words. "I saw it."

"You saw us create something beautiful. Everything has an end, but it's what happens in between that makes a life a life." Connor tugged at her right hand, cursed again, then grabbed the correct one. He tried to balance the ring box on his knee, but when it slipped, Patrick knelt down to hold it out for his cousin. Connor closed his eyes, prayed silently, and then grasped the ring between two fingers, hand shaking. "Elizabeth, will you marry me?"

"We have to help Augustus," was all she could think to say.

Connor's face fell, but then he laughed. "Lizzy, we don't have to stop helping."

"Oh."

"No? Did you say no?'

"No, I said..." Connor might have fumbled the start, but she was fumbling the finish. And why? Because she thought she could prevent it? Save them both?

There was no saving either of them from what awaited, but Connor was right. It was what happened in between that made a life a life.

"I'm saying yes, Connor." Elizabeth stretched her fingers out and let him slip the ring on. It took several tries, and was a size too big, but that was a solvable problem. *Focus on those, Lizzy. The solvable problems make the unsolvable easier to live with.*

Connor leapt to his feet and swept Elizabeth off hers, and they stayed that way, spinning in joy, in promise, in courage, to the sound of a hundred hands clapping.

AUGUSTUS DROVE HOME FROM THE OFFICE USING THE back roads. St. Charles, or even his own street, Prytania, was quicker, but the drivers faster and less attentive than the ones on Chestnut, even if he did have to stop every block. He'd checked Anasofiya's car seat three times, as he always did when leaving DMG. Two weeks she'd been joining him in the office each day, and he was starting to get the hang of the routine. He was especially proud of himself today, for attending Elizabeth's graduation *and* spending time in the office.

He made the turn on Eighth, toward Prytania and Magnolia Grace, when a truck took an illegal turn, barreling right toward the side of his car. Augustus whipped the wheel hard enough to avoid impact, but the car spun twice in the middle of the intersection before coming to a stop against the curb. Augustus hardly had time to catch his breath before one panicked word appeared in his mind.

Ana.

Augustus slammed his car door wide. Cars whizzed by, several feet away, on Prytania, but he hardly noticed them. He opened Ana's door with his breath held. She was fine. Didn't seem to have any idea that they'd very nearly *died*, as a result of that foolish, careless driver, whose license plate he wished he'd recorded to memory so he could show up at the man's door, and—

Connor appeared behind him. "Augustus? What's going on? Why is your car half in the road?"

Augustus threw his keys at him and bundled Ana in his arms, running for the safety of Magnolia Grace, where nothing could harm her.

Except, there were a hundred things in Magnolia Grace that could harm her.

A thousand in the yard.

A million in the city.

Augustus' entire body tingled, pulsing with nervous energy that stole his breath away and left stars dancing before his eyes. He raced up the stairs and only when he was safely in his bedroom did he start to breathe again, clutching Ana to his shoulder as fresh tears pricked the back of his eyes.

But even safe, he couldn't breathe. His chest was on fire with sharp pain, and he couldn't slow his pulse, no matter how he focused on steadying himself. His adrenaline surged through his veins, and though he hadn't slept well in days, he was hyper alert now, to the point everything around him was in crisp, vivid color, and the world was dripping with an abundance of unwelcome energy.

"Aggie." Elizabeth stood in the doorway.

"Go away."

"Nope. Not doing it." She came in and closed the door. "You say you don't need anyone, but that's bullshit, and we both know it." She sat next to him on the bed and held out her arms. "Give her to Aunt Elizabeth."

"No."

"Augustus."

He didn't know he was sobbing until he tasted the tears that reached his lips. "I can't."

"You can." She touched his hand. "I would die before I let anything harm a hair on her head."

"*Please,*" he sobbed, though he didn't know who the words were for. Himself. Her. God.

Elizabeth gently peeled Anasofiya away and gathered the bundle into her arms. "Shh. That's a sweet baby. Auntie Liz is here."

Arms empty, Augustus was hollow. He felt the residue of where his daughter was moments ago, where his meaning lived. He was empty. He was tired. He was *so* tired, more than he'd ever been, in all his life.

"I want you to sleep," Elizabeth said softly, but it was a demand, not a suggestion. "I want you to sleep until your body tells you it's time to do something else. In the meantime, I've got this. I've got Ana. I've got you. *Sleep*, Augustus."

Elizabeth didn't wait for his protest. She left him, closing the door again behind her.

"Thank you," he whispered, hoarse and humbled. And now, alone, for the first time in months.

He'd held firmly to the belief he and he alone navigated this new landscape as a single father, but all along, he'd had people holding him up. Elizabeth. Connor. Irish Colleen. His staff at DMG.

He was wrong, when he said he didn't need anyone.

Augustus fell asleep curled in a loose ball, his tears drenched through the knees of his bespoke trousers.

SUMMER 1976

NEW ORLEANS, LOUISIANA
VACHERIE, LOUISIANA
CAMBRIDGE, MASSACHUSETTS

CHAPTER 6
There is Love

David Allemande sat across from Augustus wearing a look of complete disbelief.

"Apologies, sir, but I do need to hear you say it again. I don't think I heard you right."

"You heard me right," Augustus said. He tapped his foot against the carpet. Today was the first in months he didn't bring Anasofiya with him to the office, and to say he was anxious didn't begin to describe the utter sense of dread that formed in his toes and permeated, through his veins, into every inch of his tired body. "I'm taking a sabbatical, David. My reasons are my own, but I expect it will last at least through this summer and into fall. Perhaps longer. I need someone I can trust implicitly to maintain my vision and direction while I'm gone."

David's eyes dropped to his hands, then to the desk, the corner, as he processed this. Augustus could imagine what he was thinking. Augustus Deschanel, the consummate control freak, overachiever, who never turned himself off. Who worked into the evening, sometimes letting night bridge to morning. David wasn't even one of the first employees, who'd seen Deschanel Media Group, and Deschanel Magazine—as well as two new magazines, launching in the fall—first hit the local grocery shelves and then take off so quickly that it was now in circulation in all fifty states, as well as three Canadian provinces.

But David Allemande lacked a critical attribute, one that Augustus, for the most part, also lacked: sentimentality. Those from the early days couldn't help but think of the magazine with a fondness that had no place in business. Augustus was proud of all he'd built, but it was a product, no more, no less. Only when it came to his staff did he soften. For them, he would've taken a loss, to protect them from even a month where they struggled to pay bills.

David could be ruthless when needed, and wouldn't hesitate to expand, where others would exercise caution. There were some who'd question his decision to leave the business in the hands of a man who'd been with the company under a year; others who'd take the choice as a slight. But Augustus didn't elevate one to punish another. His decisions could be taken at face value.

"I don't know what to say, sir."

"No need to demur with me, David. You and I both know competence and tenure aren't necessarily correlative. You see things the way I do. You, more than anyone, have understood the vision I have for DMG, and you won't hesitate when needed, but also won't jump farther than you should."

"Sir."

"My handoff to you, and back to me, should feel seamless to the rest of the employees."

"Of course, sir."

"You'll also respect that when I come back, I'd like for things to be as they were. A simple, no-fuss resumption of leadership."

David nodded. "No one would have it any other way."

Augustus stood and rebuttoned his sport coat. "This business will belong to my daughter someday. I intend to leave her something bigger than both of us."

David smiled, taking Augustus' hand in a hearty shake. "In the meantime, sir, take your time with Ana. Everything will be just as you expect it when you return."

"Better, I hope," Augustus said, as he walked David out and kept walking, toward the elevators that would take him to the lobby, the street, and, around the corner in DMG's private garage, to his car. He couldn't wait to be rid of the constrictive clothing he once wore like a second skin; the itch of the Brooks Brothers wool was relentless, the heat trapped under his starched collar stifling him. The soft silk pajamas Elizabeth bought him for Christmas beckoned, his feet crying out for the moment he'd be rid of the cloying weight of his Johnston & Murphy Oxfords.

It was summer, but maybe he'd start a fire. Ana liked watching the flames dance, as he read to her from Dickens, or sometimes Tolstoy.

Chelsea promised discretion. When she first suggested Landry's, Maureen balked. They both knew Maureen couldn't be seen at such an establishment, with heathen dock-workers and hatchery men with no loyalty to the Deschanels, and no reason to keep their mouths closed. But Chelsea patiently explained that their lack of loyalty to the Deschanels meant they had little time for them, and most wouldn't recognize one sitting across from them. *Their wives, maybe, who read the gossip rags. But these men? They have no time for anything that doesn't bring money into their house or fire in their belly. Besides, Maureen, they may not be from your world, but that doesn't mean they don't come from a world with honor.*

Chelsea was better than this too, though she went to great pains to shrug off whatever fine reputation she possessed through being a Sullivan. She dressed like she was working at the bar under less reputable intentions and swore more than any man Maureen had ever known.

But Chelsea was good on her word about keeping things discreet. Landry's had a private room, for parties. Maureen couldn't imagine what the riff-raff who drank there had to celebrate, but Chelsea, less politely, reminded her that their clientele were police, firemen, foremen... men who lived as hard as they worked and loved as hard as they lived. The back room at Landry's was booked every Friday and Saturday through winter.

The arranged meeting was set for a Tuesday afternoon, so the back room was all Maureen's, Chelsea said. Not even Mason knew the score.

Maureen followed Chelsea around, spewing out question after question as Chelsea cleaned the bar and waited for the clock to tick down. Was he handsome? What did he smell like? Was he young or old? Did he have any terrible habits? Was he terribly boring?

Chelsea sighed through each of them, and said, only, *would I set you up with a loser, Maureen Deschanel? How can I live vicariously through you if your lover is an old, crusty goblin?*

They picked a table in the corner of the room, near the glass case containing all of Mason's myriad sports trophies. There were several dozen, at least. Football, wrestling, track. Maureen wondered when he'd had time to woo Chelsea.

"We're early," Maureen said.

"He's late."

Maureen didn't drink, but needed one. This was starting all wrong. Hiding in the back of a proletarian bar in the Channel, waiting for a man who couldn't even be bothered to be on time!

"What did you tell him about me?" Maureen's voice dropped to a whisper, as if he might walk in any time and hear every word.

"Don't worry, I didn't tell him how damn neurotic you are."

"I am *not*."

Chelsea glanced meaningfully at Maureen's fingers, tapping the table in rising staccato.

"I mean, but does he know... *why* we're meeting?"

"Does he know you're looking for a discreet fuck buddy?"

"Lower your voice!"

Chelsea shook her head. She reached into her pants pocket for a pack of cigarettes and shook one out. "Yeah, Maureen, he knows. I made sure he was interested in this before I told him anything at all about you."

"So you did tell him about me."

"Only your situation," Chelsea said. "And even then, only what he needed to know."

"Which is?"

"That your marriage isn't a traditional one and you're looking for a discreet lover. Oh, and that he didn't need to worry about your husband coming around wielding a bat, because you had his approval."

Maureen buried her head in her hands. "What he must think of me. I'm a *mother*, Chels. Did you know Olivia now says *mama*? I wonder if she'll learn *adulterer* next."

Chelsea perked at the sound of the bells announcing a visitor in the bar beyond. "That'll be him, probably. And look, there's a reason I suggested Soren. You're not the only one whose life isn't what you pictured. If anyone knows about non-traditional, it's a LaViolette who's too far removed from the heir's line to be valuable, but too close to ever be free. I guess your equivalent of a Guidry."

Chelsea stubbed out her cigarette and went to retrieve their guest.

Now that Augustus was on his formal leave from work, it was harder and harder to convince him to let Elizabeth take Ana for a bit. What finally swayed him was her insistence that she wasn't doing it only to help; she *wanted* to hold her niece and bond with her. She rather liked the little one, despite usually finding babies bothersome.

Augustus didn't fight too hard about Elizabeth and Connor moving in formally, either. He'd helped Evangeline, once, and was happy to do the same for his baby sister. He didn't know she wasn't planning to go to college, and that was news she intended to keep to herself for now.

Connor, on the other hand, couldn't contain his excitement for his own fall enrollment at Tulane, where nearly all Sullivans started, and usually finished, their college journeys. She was excited *for* him, dulled only by the knowledge that just because she didn't intend to go didn't mean she didn't want to. One more curse of her gift, keeping her from a life experience everyone else was preparing for while Elizabeth tried to decide just what profession she could take on that would offer the most mental and emotional peace. It didn't make this decision easier, knowing once she came into her trust she'd never need to work a day in her life. Her trust, like her visions, was a gift she'd never asked for.

The wet nurse stopped by every evening to drop off fresh milk. Lacy was lithe and blond, and reminded Elizabeth a bit of Ekatherina, but if Augustus noted this, he made no point of it. When Elizabeth called out, with some ulterior motive, that Lacy seemed to have a small crush on the master of Magnolia Grace, Augustus damn near took her head off.

"Jesus, Lizzy, you sound like Mama, you know that? You think another woman is anywhere near registering on my list of priorities right now?"

"Um, well—"

"Right now or ever," he finished. "As for Lacy... stop projecting your own feelings onto her, will you? She's been a godsend. I don't want to lose her services."

"Sheesh. Yes, sir." She didn't bring it up again, and instead focused on how to construct a routine for all of them that even he could live with.

Augustus built, at Elizabeth's request, an enclosure around the broad back porch at Magnolia Grace. Summers in New Orleans were too hot for infants, but with the netting of the screen and the four fans running overhead, it was perfect for Ana, who seemed somehow drawn to the sun, just as she was to fire.

Elizabeth rocked her niece against her chest, sipping the iced tea Connor delivered. He'd added another flavor. Lavender, she thought, although flowers had no place in anyone's food, as far as she was concerned. It wasn't bad. Connor, she was learning, as they bridged the journey from kids who had others to care for them to adults responsible for their own selves, was decent in the kitchen. His mother only had boys, and Savannah Normand Sullivan was determined *someone* would carry on her recipes; her passion. With her cancer in remission, she'd been even more dedicated to documenting the culinary family traditions, making sure both her twin sons took this process with the gravity it deserved.

Irish Colleen hadn't let any of her kids near the kitchen, and if any of them turned out to be decent with a spatula, this was purely coincidental.

Ana stirred against Elizabeth's neck, slipping in and out of her baby sleep.

Elizabeth was rocked with an immediate, powerful vision.

A series of images, one after the other. No clarity, only snapshots in time.

Anasofiya, no more than a toddler, in a full body cast, Augustus pleading with her to do something.

Anasofiya, sobbing over a silver frame that held a picture of a mother she'd never meet.

Anasofiya, as a preteen, lying under a broad oak tree with Nicolas as he played with her vibrant red hair.

Anasofiya, blushing as her father slipped a corsage over her wrist.

Anasofiya, holding hands with a young man—had to be a Sullivan, with his black hair, green eyes, and Sullivan jawline—as she walked down Prytania, magnolia trees in full bloom.

Anasofiya, hovering in a dark bar in a part of town not her own, waiting.

Anasofiya, lifted from the cold ocean.

Anasofiya, bleeding out on someone's kitchen floor.

Anasofiya, fighting against the love building in her heart as she watched a beautiful blond man sleep.

Anasofiya, running away from that same man, heart breaking.

Anasofiya, holding her son for the first time.

Elizabeth surged forward so hard she had to wrap her arms tight around Ana to prevent her from flying, too. Her breaths came ragged and fast, too fast to catch up and steady herself. She rarely had visions like these. Hers were tied to single events, usually playing out like a movie, not a montage. What was this? Would she see more? Was she evolving?

And why now? Why with Ana, who was still so new to the world?

"Sweet girl," Elizabeth whispered against her niece's bright hair. She'd stopped rocking, but her body trembled. "It's okay, sweet girl."

A shadow fell over her, dropping several feet before her on the flagstones. "I'll take her now."

Elizabeth let him peel Ana from her arms. She resumed rocking. Thinking.

"Not gonna argue this time?"

Elizabeth ground her hands into the rocker to hide the trembles. "Nope."

CHAPTER 7
Bicentennial

A stir of activity whizzed by Charles at the top of the steps to the second floor. "What the hell are you doing?"

"Moving back in," Cordelia said casually. She demanded Richard and his staff take her bags back to the heir's suite before Charles had a chance to put his foot down.

"I'm sorry... *why*?"

"It's my house?"

Charles descended a step. "It's my house, but if you mean in the way anything that belongs to the husband belongs to the wife, it's still my house. Didn't you read the prenup? Why the fuck are you here?"

"Our son deserves a nuclear family."

Charles snorted. "Our son is thriving without your bullshit."

"Be that as it may," Cordelia said, as she draped the strap of her purse over the hooks in the hallway. "He is my son."

Charles went down another couple steps as two more bags made their way past him. He had half a mind to stop it, but he was more curious about Cordelia than angry. For now. "What are you playing at?"

"Simply, that I've had time to think about this, and while I have no intention for us to take up as any *normal* couple would, our son should feel the daily presence of both parents. Not very unlike what Maureen is doing, after that loveless marriage you arranged for her, no?"

"You don't talk about my family," Charles said, a new edge coming to his voice. "Nicolas doesn't need both of us here to thrive. He needs stability." He dropped down another step. "What he needs is love, and you're not capable of it."

If Cordelia was wounded by the assertion, she showed no signs. "He's too young to know the history between us."

"By history, you must mean having your insides ripped out so he can't have any brothers or sisters."

"Or how you murdered my father. I could've meant that, too."

"Your father was a rapist," Charles countered. "A *child* rapist."

"And Nicolas will have his siblings, when your little French tart proves out her fertility, no doubt."

"She's sleeping in the bed with me, so you'll have to find another suite to call headquarters to your satanic franchise."

Cordelia took his chin in her bony fingers. "Oh, come on, Charles. We both know Satan would never franchise. Now. Where's my son?"

"With Lisette. He's getting ready for his aunt to pick him up for the celebrations in the Quarter."

"What celebrations?"

"While you were busy boiling virgins and plucking out the eyes of poor bayou toads, our country turned two hundred years old. Don't suppose you noticed that every goddamn building in this town is decorated in red, white, and blue?"

"The bicentennial," Cordelia said, nodding. "Celebrating the day the ungrateful rebels decided they'd rather pay taxes to a heathen government than remain connected to the esteemed and noble European establishment that might've redeemed their Godless, classless souls."

"Yeah. Anyway." Charles gave her the look he gave crazies. "He's going. Soon."

"Soon isn't now," Cordelia replied and ascended the stairs in the direction of the nursery.

"I NEED HELP."

Evangeline hadn't ever said the words before, and once they were out, she wondered why. There was power in admitting vulnerability. Even strength. The words freed her, at least of the burden of living with them.

"Evie, I can be on a plane in—"

"No, Leena. It's not like that, this time. I need advice."

"Oh," Colleen replied. She shuffled around on her side, and it sounded like she was settling in. "What kind of advice?"

"Are you following the news in Massachusetts?"

"Things have been rather hectic around here, with Amelia, and trying to get everything with the Collective sorted before we fly back to Scotland for fall term. Noah, her bottle is getting too hot. Can you pull it down?" Colleen sighed. "I'm so sorry. You didn't call to hear me get distracted on you."

"It's fine, but we have a killer targeting college kids in Cambridge, and I don't know what to do about it."

The busy sounds from Colleen's end came to an abrupt halt. For a moment, there was only silence. "What did you just say?"

"He's killed twelve girls, Colleen. Four more are missing." Evangeline swallowed. "I knew one of them. Leanne Berringer. We're in the same program and have two classes together." She looked out the window of her apartment, the one facing the brick façade of campus. "*Had.*"

"Evangeline." Colleen's words came out breathless, almost a whisper. "How the hell did I miss this? Twelve girls?"

"Like you said, you've been busy," Evangeline replied. "And sixteen, really. Fact is, he doesn't let them live, and the ones who went missing most recently are beyond the threshold of any hopeful recovery."

"You sound like an expert, and that breaks my heart."

"He rapes them, Colleen. Over and over. And then he strangles them with their own clothing. Their nylons, or scarves, or knee socks. Every one."

"Evie." Colleen shuffled around in the background. "Wait, maybe I did hear something about this. But I thought it was Washington. Or Utah."

"That's another guy."

"Is it? Evangeline, what if it *is* the same guy?"

"That guy, the one you're talking about, he, uh... he's also a necrophile. Ours only does it when they're alive."

"Dear God."

"Colleen, they can't seem to catch him. I don't know why. I'm not a cop. But what I do know is that we're all terrified, and every time I hear about another girl going missing, I relive what happened to me in that warehouse over and over and over again. I've tried using logic to tell myself it's not going to happen to me, that I'm safe, but I'm *not* safe. No young college women in Cambridge are safe right now, and I'm spiraling."

Colleen absorbed this instead of responding immediately. Evangeline appreciated her restraint, because Colleen's natural inclination was to go into solve mode when someone presented a problem. Evangeline didn't want platitudes. She needed practical advice, and when in the right frame of mind, Colleen was good with that, too.

"You want control," Colleen said. "No, you need it."

Evangeline nodded into the phone. She wound the cord around her hand so tight the color of her flesh turned white.

"I understand why this situation feels like your power is being taken from you," Colleen said.

"Yes."

Colleen lowered her voice. "So. You take it back."

FOUR STROLLERS. THREE ADULTS.

Olivia, mostly through body language and a few words

peppered into half-sentences, made it clear that, at fifteen months, she didn't *need* a stroller, thank you very much. Maureen mouthed the words, *oh yes she does*, over her daughter's head as she handed her off to Colleen. Earlier, while Maureen packed the diaper bag, she told Colleen that Olivia was already a handful. "For my sins. I think I'm getting ready to raise myself, Colleen. She's all sass, no sense."

Colleen let Olivia, the oldest of the cousins, stand at her side during the parade, their little secret. Nicolas, Anasofiya, and Amelia lay in a parallel line in their strollers, in various stages of sleep and curiosity as the activities rolled by.

Noah positioned himself between Nicolas and Amelia, alternately checking in on each of them, while Elizabeth hovered protectively over Anasofiya. In her fear over Augustus' obsessive state, she'd absorbed some of these behaviors for herself. Her eyes conveyed the possibility that anyone, at any time, could harm her niece, and she'd hardly relaxed at all since they arrived. Colleen was surprised Elizabeth even managed to get Ana sprung from the house at all.

The Brother Martin band passed by playing "Three Cheers for the Red, White, and Blue" in their colorful, patriotic uniforms. Colleen and Noah clapped and sang along as they leaned into the strollers, enjoying the wonder on the faces of the little ones. Olivia clapped, too, but kept losing her balance, so Colleen knelt, taking her hands in hers, and they clapped together.

"Three cheers for the red, white, and blue! Or the red is the blood of our broooothers," they sang, and Colleen remembered how both Charles and Augustus went to Brother Martin. Augustus, through graduation. Charles, until he was kicked out. Neither had been in a band, but Charles did play the drums for a month before losing interest.

Signs everywhere, hanging from poles and dangling from power lines, in bold cursive, announced the two-hundredth anniversary of the United States of America. Vendors were set up on every corner, selling patches, T-shirts, banners, and other memorabilia Colleen imagined would sit on shelves for years to come. *The Spirit of 76. Happy Birthday Liberty. 1776-1976. Take Your Tea and Shove It.* All variety of slogans, in storefront windows, in the backs of cars. Mayor Schiro blocked off the Quarter on all sides, allowing only store traffic in or out of the quadrant from the river to Canal, from Esplanade to North Rampart. The St. Charles Streetcar was so packed they'd had to wait three cars for one that had room.

The Preservation Hall group was next, and they played their trumpets, horns, and clarinets with zeal, as everyone around erupted into *When the Saints Go Marching In.*

"Oh when those Saints!" the singers yelled, and the crowd responded, "Oh, when those Saints!"

"Go marching in!"

"Go marching in!'

Noah disappeared for about fifteen minutes and returned to a group of baton twirlers doing their routine to "I Wish I Was in Dixieland."

"I wish I was in Dixie! Hooray! Hooray!" sang the crowd, enthusiasm building with every word.

Colleen accepted the cool drink from her husband, as he handed the other to Elizabeth. "Nothing like a little Dixie to get the Southerners animated," she joked.

"I suspect some are wishing they were still there."

"Some?" Elizabeth raised both cynical brows. "Look at these old men, slapping their knees and singing about cotton, dreaming about all the ways they could've turned the tide and won the War of Northern Aggression."

"It's the moonshine," Noah said, giving her a soft elbow. "Kills brain cells."

"Racism kills brain cells."

Colleen shook her head. "We'll raise our children to be better than that. I'd like to think the farther we get from monstrous acts, the better we are."

"History tells us otherwise," Elizabeth said, rolling Anasofiya back and forth. "Humans are always monsters, we just do better from time to time, and when the low bar is genocide, well, anything looks decent."

Noah examined his Coca-Cola. "Maybe I should have upgraded to beer for this conversation."

Olivia tapped Colleen's leg. She looked down, and the little girl was pointing at her red can.

"Better not, sweet thing. Your mother would kill me."

"You think those are the wide eyes of someone who's seen a Coke for the first time?" Elizabeth quipped. "Someone's been sneaking that kid some junk food."

"When I look at her, it's like looking at a baby Maureen," Colleen mused. "They could be twins."

"Thank God she doesn't look like her father," Elizabeth said.

"Hey, why didn't Maureen come with us today?" Noah asked.

"I'm not real sure," Colleen replied. "She said she was meeting someone, but didn't say who or what about."

Elizabeth snickered to herself.

Nicolas started slapping his feet against the stroller, making grunting sounds. Colleen lifted him from the stroller, and he wiggled until she let him down on the pavement, where he immediately found strong footing. He bucked to the music, laughing, emoting what Charles called his "baby language," a series of incomprehensible syllables that seemed to make complete sense to Nicolas, and no one else. He talked to himself, to his toys, to his cousins, entire conversations, but nothing he said was a word anyone recognized. Charles told her only geniuses make up languages, like that guy who wrote *Lord of the Rings.*

Tolkien?

Eh?

The man who wrote... never mind.

Nicolas squealed as a float of Uncle Sam, decked in rich red, white, blue, silver, and gold, rolled by. Beads of the same colors flew from the top, and one landed at his feet.

"Dada!" he cried, and all three adults whipped their necks around.

"What did you say?" Colleen asked him.

Nicolas bent to pick up the beads, but Noah was quicker. "Captain Germ Away is here to save the day!"

Elizabeth rolled her eyes.

"Dada!" Nicolas cried, reaching for the beads.

"Should we tell him?" Colleen asked. "He'll be so happy!"

Elizabeth shook her head. "Better to pretend when he hears it for the first time that it's really his first word. His ego can't handle his sisters hearing it first."

"True," Colleen said. She looked at Noah. "I think he wants those beads for his father."

Noah smiled and slipped them into his pocket. "We'll wash them up, then, so he can give them to Dada."

CHAPTER 8

Old Souls

Soren LaViolette was a fascinating human, and this was not a word Maureen could recall ever using about anyone before him. It wasn't a word she used about anything, really, because it seemed to her the kind of description you reserved for something really spectacular. People liked to waste big words on little things, and then when something really interesting —*fascinating*—happened, there were no words left.

He was a twenty-six-year-old out-of-work poet, and when she repeated those words aloud to herself before the gilt mirror her father bought her when she was a little girl—one of the few things she insisted on bringing with her to Blanchard House, other than clothing—they didn't leave her with a swell of pride in her choice.

But Soren was so much more than that!

He'd tried to work, but his aunt, Ruth Ann, the dowager heir of the LaViolette clan, was responsible for approving all careers within the family. Maureen made Soren repeat that a few times, because this was insane to Maureen, who was no stranger to having at least some curation of her life as a Deschanel, but had always been told she could be whatever she wanted. *You mean you can't choose what you want to do with your life*? she asked. He explained, weary, that those in the heir's line have no choice at all.

They were appointed to a skill that benefited the family—judges, bankers, politicians. Outside the heir's line, they could choose from a broader list, but it still had to be approved and blessed. And if they chose none? Then they must live quietly, and in a sort of exile. That was the life Soren had elected, when the options laid before him were more a choice in which prison to lock himself into.

That's completely bonkers, she'd said, and then kissed him, their first kiss, and she knew it would not be their last. She'd never done anything like that before; even when selling her services as the virginity thief, she'd commanded the men to make each move, guiding them through the steps while never initiating.

Soren's mother, Rosebud, gifted him her weekend home in Bayou St. John, close enough to come visit her, far enough as to keep him out of the sights of his aunt, who led the family with exacting precision and left no trace when dealing with their enemies... which included those sharing her blood.

"If you think being a branch off the heir's line is devaluing, try being a man in a clan where only the women matter," he said, but didn't elaborate. Maureen had heard things over the years about this family, and his words didn't surprise her.

But Soren was the antithesis of what Maureen knew about the cunning LaViolettes.

He was creative, sensitive, thoughtful. When she talked about herself, he didn't wait for her to finish so he could speak. He listened, and when he did talk, it was to ask more, to dig deeper. To know her seemed very important to Soren.

On their first meeting at the house in Bayou St. John, they did no more than talk and kiss. On the second, Soren asked her about her marriage.

"Why, so you can write about it?" Maureen hissed, but she smiled at the edge of the words and kicked him with her bare foot, legs stretched across his lap. She hardly knew him, and yet was comfortable enough to let her guard down.

"Do you want me to write about it?" Soren took her feet

firmly in his hands and ran his thumbs over her arches. She shivered.

"Do you want to write about it?"

"Do you want me to want you to want me to write about it?"

Maureen giggled and tried to free her feet, but he grinned and yanked, knocking her back against the couch. "You read a lot. I'm sure there's already hundreds of books about a beautiful young woman cursed in marriage to an old fuddy-duddy."

"Thousands, even," Soren replied, eyes twinkling. "But most end with that same beautiful young woman softening the time-hardened heart of the old fuddy-duddy and finding love in their differences."

Maureen wrinkled her face. "Yeah, that's not my marriage."

"Because of you, or him?"

Maureen successfully withdrew her feet from his vice grip, but on second thought, slid them back over. She liked the velvety softness of his hands on her flesh; his gentle, but assertive control. "The truth is, Soren... he doesn't want me."

Soren didn't ply her with overdone protestations. He instead watched her, thoughtful. "He must have odd tastes, then."

"What makes you say that?"

"You already know you're beautiful, Maureen. So does he. Maybe he enjoys the company of men?"

Maureen snorted. "Edouard? No."

"Don't look so scandalized. It's not as uncommon as you think. Men, especially, feel compelled to keep their homosexuality a secret. We like to say we live in a free country, but that's only true for some."

"Just trust me. He's not into men."

"Then trust me and tell me."

Tell me. She'd never told anyone, at least not all of it. Chelsea had heard pieces, her sisters yet others, but she'd told no one the entire, sordid tale. To do so risked both her reputation, and also exposed the most horrible day of her life... the day that turned *into* her life.

Trust me.

If not him, then who? And why not?

So she did. Maureen told Soren everything, every last detail.

Soren listened without interrupting. Only when she was done did he say, "He was wrong to hurt you, Maureen. I'm so sorry."

"I don't want *pity,* you just said to tell—"

Soren silenced her with a kiss. "It's not pity. Just acknowledgment that what happened to you was unfair. And wrong. I suspect I'm still right about him."

"Even after all that, you think he's into men?"

Soren shrugged. He ran his hands across her ankles, tracing shapes with his fingertips. "The only way he can get off is through extreme measures. There's nothing wrong with sadomasochism, but if he has no interest in sex without that control and degradation, then it's possible this is due to him being in denial about what, and who, really gets him off." Soren gave her ankle a quick squeeze. "Whatever he's got brewing inside him, Maureen, it's not about you. And it's not something you can fix by being more beautiful, or more desirable." He touched his hand to his lips, and then her ankle once more. "Even if that were possible."

Maureen had never considered her husband in quite this way. A part of her understood that it wasn't about her, but she'd still convinced herself that if she was more beautiful, or more desirable, she might be able to change him. "How do you know all this?"

"I spend most of my life watching the world around me," Soren replied. Outside a cloud passed overhead and the room was momentarily bathed in muted light. His brilliant golden hair was now simply blond; his cerulean eyes merely blue. "But that's a writer for you. Nothing we write is original, just our version of things."

"So you think I'm a fool for trying to make him love me."

"No, Maureen. I don't think you're a fool at all." Soren smiled, a gesture that animated his whole face. "Him, maybe. But if he wasn't a fool, your feet wouldn't be in my lap, would they?"

"I bet you say that to all the girls."

His expression darkened. "There haven't been that many."

"I showed you mine," Maureen said with a flippant nod. "Your turn."

"My family drives them away. They're either too poor, or too average, or too *less than* whatever my mother and aunt feel is best for me. Or, really, best for the family, seeing as we care more about our reputation than our emotional well-being." Soren's hands went still. "They know about you, if you're wondering."

"So soon? But how?"

"They don't miss anything," Soren replied. "Just as your family knows about us."

Maureen's eyes widened. "We only just met." A thousand scenarios of her deepest secrets revealed danced through the space of a single thought. "There's no way my family knows. I've been completely discreet."

Soren shrugged. "Does it matter? They'll leave us alone. Mine will because they know you have just as much to lose if the truth comes out, and if they keep me at least somewhat satisfied, then I'm not a liability. Yours will because they already meddled in your life once."

Way more than once. "Somewhat satisfied?"

Soren watched her with a whimsical look. "I just met you and I already know you'll satisfy one part of me. But everyone has something that has to be just for them."

"Like your poetry."

"Yes," he said. He looked as if there was more, but he left it at that.

"But..." Maureen considered her words very carefully, as they came to her. "You write your poetry now. Don't you?"

"I have to hide it away from the world. Same as you have to hide who you are."

Maureen balked. "What the hell does that mean?"

"You're a Deschanel."

"And?" Maureen's heart rate surged.

Soren's only response was a wry smile.

"Look—"

Soren rolled forward. "I know because we can do things, too."

"What? Who is we?"

"My family."

Could he be telling the truth? "Prove it."

Soren sighed. He lifted one hand in the air and with a bored look, summoned his drink from the kitchen and into his palm. He slurped the dark liquid through a straw, never taking his eyes off her.

Maureen was astonished.

"I showed you mine," he said playfully.

She was too shocked to respond appropriately. Here was someone, someone not related to her, who was a witch! Someone who could do what her family could do and wasn't the least bit bothered by it. She never *dreamed* anything like this was possible, let alone so close to her. The same city, the same circles. That the universe would connect them, in a world where billions went about their lives entirely in the dark to magic...

"Maureen?"

"I..." she exhaled. Dizzy. Overcome. "I can't show you mine."

"And why not?"

"It's broken."

Soren laughed. "Broken?"

"It's not funny."

"Then explain it to me."

Maureen drew her feet back, tucking them under her. She ignored his wounded look, too overwhelmed to explain it wasn't about him, that what she'd explored to satisfy her needs had turned into so much more... something far harder to define. "I used to be able to talk to the dead. It went away when... well, I'm not entirely sure, but I think when I married Edouard and became the mistress of Blanchard House. I couldn't talk to all of them. Just some of them. I don't know why. I never had time to learn the rules, and then it was gone."

"What an incredible gift that must have been," he mused. "But also unsettling."

"It was both," she agreed. "Wonderful and terrible. There were so many times I wanted it to go away, and then when it did..." She hesitated not from emotion, but from the sudden realization that this conversation was *really happening*. Someone who was not her blood relative had revealed his own supernatural gifts, and a discussion was taking place about them. Never in all her wildest fantasies did the idea of meeting someone like her ever appear. Waking up one day a princess in a foreign land seemed far more feasible than meeting another witch.

That she should meet such a person when she was already married seemed so unfair.

"I'm sorry," Soren said. "I've never known anyone who lost their ability."

"Me neither," Maureen said, breathless. She needed to get ahold of herself; to be as calm as he apparently was. "How did you know about me?"

"I knew about your family," he amended. "Because my family knew."

This seemed like the kind of thing the Deschanels ought to know. Maureen made a mental note to tell Colleen later about this, but she'd forget to do this, as she forgot most things she told herself to remember later.

"Is that why you agreed to meet me?"

Soren inched closer and rested his head against her shoulder. "I suppose I thought if there was anyone else in the world who might understand isolation and loneliness, it would be someone from a family like mine."

"It's time, isn't it?" Noah asked, though it wasn't a question at all. Colleen appreciated his delicate phrasing. He didn't normally treat her so gently, but he seemed to know when to ease into a subject rather than barrel through.

"Soon," she replied. She watched Amelia sleep in her cradle. Amelia, with the white hair, that so few Deschanels had. Anymore, at least. The white-blond hair was a signature trait of the French Deschanels, but somewhere the genes dwindled from their makeup, choosing to make scattered appearances. Next to Nicolas, with his dark chestnut waves, and Anasofiya, with her wispy strands like fire, it was as if they were made to represent the entire Deschanel spectrum. It made Colleen wish she understood more about her ancestry beyond the proud French roots. Surely other backgrounds had married into the family many times over the years, but no one talked about them.

Would Amelia outgrow it? Some babies did, but Colleen could see her daughter clearly, as a teen, as a woman, hair still as pale as her skin.

And what gift has our bloodline given you, *dear one?*

"Fall term, then," Noah said. "It'll be a cleaner start for both our programs."

Colleen nodded. "Catherine is due in late summer. We can check in on her and the baby on our way back."

"I wonder... you know... what Amelia will be able to do," Noah mused, a hint of controlled caution in his voice.

"To do?"

"Her... gift."

"Like my healing you mean?"

"Like that."

"I was just wondering the same actually."

"When will we know?"

Colleen shrugged and played with the edges of Amelia's thin blanket. Noah was trying, and his attempts weren't forced anymore, just unsure. This world was new to him, and he was finding his footing. Anything other than patience from her would be unfair. "I don't know. There's so many different gifts in the family, and as far as I can tell, it's not like other genetic markers where a child of healers is more likely to be one. I suspect that the marker is only the propensity for *a* gift, not an indication of who will be given what. But no one really knows, because everything we know about ourselves comes from within the family. Our knowledge is insular."

Noah frowned in contemplation. "When did you know?"

Colleen withdrew her hand and leaned back into the rocker Kellan bought her for nursing Amelia. "I'm not entirely sure, because my mother, back then, acted like our gifts were courtesy of Satan and forbade us from using them. My father, who was like Augustus, didn't discourage us, but he didn't really teach us about ourselves, either. But..." Colleen rocked and closed her eyes, falling into the memory. "My first clear image of myself healing had to be at about three. I don't think I was four yet, because it was around my fourth birthday that Dad moved us from Ophélie to Oak Haven, here in the Garden District, and the memory comes from Ophélie... a bit beyond the property, out in the swamp. Was just me, Mama, and Maddy, and Maddy and I were playing on a blanket while Mama was harvesting swamp cabbage and chicory—"

"Wait, your mother, one of the richest women in Louisiana, was foraging for food?"

"You've met her," Colleen said with a raised brow. "She wasn't watching Maddy and me that carefully, and Maddy was in a phase where she ran *everywhere.* All the time. Running. Well, she tripped over some cypress knees and went tumbling, hit her head on another knee, and when Mama's face went pale, something spurred to life inside me. It's hard to explain. I just... knew if I didn't do something, Maddy might be in real trouble. So I ran to her, Mama shouting after me, and I put hands on her and I felt the energy transfer. I felt the blood pooling away from her brain, and the lifelessness dissolve away. I couldn't have described it at that age, of course, but I sensed that whatever I was doing was making her better."

Noah ran his hands through his hair. "That's incredible."

Colleen wrapped the shawl around her. Even in the summer, there were spots in The Gardens that held a permanent chill. "But it's possible that happened before, and I just don't remember. Mama didn't address it at all, though I saw in her eyes she hadn't missed a single thing. She knew. But was that because I'd done it before that? I'll never know. She's never wanted to talk about who we are."

"Hearing you say that reminds me of how unfair it was for me to treat you the way I did."

"You were in shock," Colleen offered graciously, because it still hurt when she let herself pause too long on the memory. For her marriage to work, she could never pause too long in the dark places of their separation, and she suspected all marriages had these dark spots, smaller than the light but powerful if you let them in. "Mama likes to say she didn't know what she married into, but she did. She spent over a year nursing my father's first wife, and throughout that, they had family healers in and out all the time. She knew."

"Why were they ineffective? Maybe that's why she didn't believe."

Colleen gave herself a moment to think of how to describe what she was going to say next. "Consent is an integral part of the healing process. I know there are situations, like with you, where it isn't possible, but when someone *is* alert, and present, and can make decisions, if they aren't receptive to receiving what's been given, there is a sort of natural defense that kicks in to prevent the healing from taking. Ophelia always said Eliza knew it was her time, and so she fought what she believed to be unnatural."

Noah frowned. "But you were able to heal me because I was unconscious."

"I won't apologize," Colleen said, her defenses kicking up. "Don't ever ask me to. I'm glad you were out cold, because you might have fought me, and if you'd fought me you wouldn't be sitting here asking me these questions. I don't care if it's against the rules we set for ourselves as Deschanel witches. I don't care if it was wrong, Noah, I will never *ever* be sorry for it."

Noah leaned against the wall, watching her. His mouth was

curved, in seriousness, but it was soft, ready, thoughtful like his eyes. "I'm the only one who should be sorry... and always will be."

Close the box. Leave the darkness inside. He loves you more than any man has business loving a woman, and for you to harbor resentment... for him to feel forever indebted and forever inadequate in his remorse... that serves neither of you. Neither, Colleen. It will only fester, like a cancer, and destroy the beauty in what you both are.

The voice, the words, were Ophelia's, but she wasn't here anymore, and Colleen didn't know if she'd inherited the wisdom or just learned to predict it.

Colleen fought against her stubborn insistence to see him in perpetual penance. She shuffled across the carpet and folded herself into his arms.

"We won't speak of it ever again, Noah. Not my hurt. Not your regret. We have Amelia now, and we have the experience to know we never want to be where we were a year ago. The scorecard has been reset. The balance is restored. We both have to let go."

Noah's arms shook as he held her; his pain transferred, not to her, but through her, releasing itself back into the universe. He wasn't the best with words, so perhaps he'd never been capable of telling her the depth of his sorrow over his actions, but she felt it now, as she gave him permission to give it up, and herself permission to let go of her own anger and indignation at being the *one who was wronged.*

"I love you, Colleen. I can't stand the idea that I only get one lifetime with you."

Colleen pressed her lips to his heart. "If I ever find an immortal Deschanel, I'll make sure to learn their secret."

CHAPTER 9
Mama

"But she *is* his mother."

"Giving birth doesn't make you a mother."

Lisette didn't immediately respond. "I know your anger. But she came back for him. Yes? She must be remorse."

"Remorseful."

Lisette flushed. Charles had never corrected her before. He'd known doing so would be a swift, sharp reminder of who was superior in the room, and he loathed himself for the deliberate power move with someone he was supposed to love.

"Why are you taking her side, anyway?"

Lisette balked. "I am *not* on her side."

Charles rolled around in the bed, turning his back to her. "Coulda fooled me."

He felt Lisette shake her head against the pillow. "No, I think not of Mistress Deschanel and her feelings, but only of Nicolas. I worry for a child who grow up thinking their mother does not love."

This tempered Charles' swelling rage—a bit. He could see her point, even if she was wrong. "Lis. Worse things will happen if he grows up with that hellbeast for a mother. Don't you understand that? He has you, he has my mother, he has four aunts who adore him, and he will, when he gets older, have Ana, Amelia, and Olivia. He'll have an overload of female attention and love. More than he knows what to do with. If anything, there aren't enough male influences in his life to balance out all that goddamn estrogen."

Lisette made no further rebuttal, though Charles wished she would. Although he didn't agree with her, he liked to know what she thought, because having feelings about something meant she was connected to him beyond the job he'd hired her to do. Lately, he'd felt like she was pulling away from him, and closer to the work.

The next part was predictable. She excused herself to clean up and return to her work. No pillow talk for this one.

At least *someone* was on his side. Charles had met Dan Weatherly for drinks the night before at the Playboy Club, where Weatherly was still an active member. Marriage hadn't slowed him even a bit, a fact he wasn't the least ashamed of.

"I've always known she was a psychotic cunt," Dan said, finishing his first beer before Charles could even take a sip of his.

"Thanks for telling me *before* I fucking married her."

Dan popped some nuts into his mouth, crunching with his mouth open as he shrugged. "Would it have made a difference?" he asked, mouth full. "*You* knew she was a psychotic cunt and was still convinced marrying her was a rock-solid idea."

"I had my reasons." Charles' eyes scanned the crowd, looking for an easy lay. He didn't mean to do it. It came from a place of old instinct.

Dan lit a cigarette. "I remember. Some bullshit about your dad."

It wasn't bullshit. "Doesn't matter now."

"No?" Dan took a drag, leaned his head back, and blew his smoke into the hazy air. He made eye contact with someone across the room and nodded. "Then why haven't you kicked the bitch out?"

"I—"

"I mean, *really,* Charles, what the *fuck* is stopping you?"

What, indeed? Franz's blackmail died with him. Cordelia had nothing to hold over the Deschanels with her father gone, and Nicolas was born in wedlock, not out. She'd never bear him another child, and her only role now was to pretend to mother the ones Lisette would. Was he really so much like her that he cared what others thought?

I'm becoming my father.

He thought about asking Colin's advice, but conscience kept him from asking Colin a damn thing about anything until Catherine returned home safely.

Appearances only mattered when you couldn't buy your way out of problems. He didn't care what anyone thought of him rutting with the nanny when there'd never be any consequences.

Except...

Colin's wisdom appeared to him in absentia.

What if something happened to Nicolas?

That's a terrible thing to even think!

As a father, yes, it's unthinkable. As your lawyer, it's all but required.

It wouldn't matter. If something happened to Nicolas, I'd hurl myself off a bridge.

Perhaps, but then you'd require an heir more urgently.

Colin Sullivan was a stone-cold pragmatic son-of-a-bitch in his imagination.

Fine. Whatever children I have with Lisette—

Will they be born in or out of wedlock?

I—

You divorce Cordelia, you strip away your veneer of legitimacy. Unless you plan to marry Lisette?

No.

Right. Because the only thing worse than being married to a sociopath is being married to the help?

It's not like that!

Isn't it?

I have my reasons.

Your reasons are bullshit.

I didn't know you cursed!

It's your imagination.

Round and round spun his head. Round and round and round, and every time he felt convicted about a decision, round and round his thoughts took him, until he was left more confused than he'd started.

And what would his sisters say? He didn't need to come to each of them in his head. They were all some form of *leave the bitch, marry for love,* and even Augustus would have a pragmatic way of sending the same message.

As he did each and every time, Charles tabled this decision for a later time, hoping eventually these exercises would lead to clarity.

He went to seek out Nicolas for some playtime.

LUTHER FONTENOT SAT STOICALLY AT THE ELONGATED table in the Council chambers, hands folded over the mahogany, suit crisp and recently dry-cleaned, or perhaps purchased, but impeccable and overdone, even for the outlandish traditions of the Deschanel Magi Collective Council. At fifteen, he looked twice the age of the oldest person in the room, and before he said a word even, the mood shifted as everyone watched his serious, focused eyes, so light blue they were nearly gray, travel the room in intense observation.

The only giveaway to his nerves was the jagged rise and fall of his shoulders.

So young. But then, most of them were. Pierce was the only one of the Council into his middle age, and though his sister Eugenia wasn't far behind, they were still both so young for a role so vitally important to the family's safety and prosperity. Just because they'd never experienced an emergency in their lifetimes didn't mean there wouldn't be, again, as there always was where the Deschanels were concerned. Their youth was a barrier to an earlier time, but would it also be a barrier of the cyclical nature of history, which would again, if not soon, repeat itself? Would their flippant disregard of things like a family curse help or hinder them? Would they be ready?

Looking at the gravity in the gaze and demeanor of the young Luther Fontenot gave her hope.

"Thank you for coming tonight, Luther," Colleen began.

"Thank you for having me, Colleen." The only sign of his youth was the light crack of nerves running through his otherwise deep, mature voice.

Colleen, with the help of the Council, walked him through the recitation of his vows, which he was hearing for the first time. He wasn't only young to be on the Council, fifteen was also young to be a member. But she'd told him what to expect, and undoubtedly, so had his mother, Eugenia.

"This is a sacred vow," Colleen said, repeating what she'd told him before he took his vows and sealed his spot on the Council. "The most sacred that we can take. All of us have been baptized. We've taken the sacraments. These are our duties to God. But God has given us no guidance on who we are. The Bible doesn't talk about people like us, and so we make our own rules, and we look after ourselves. We have no choice."

"I understand."

"Do you?" Pansy snapped her gum, creating a parachute of pink against her lips.

"I do, Pansy." Luther gripped his hands together tighter as he scanned the room, filled with cousins, his mother, uncles. Family outside of the room, and family inside the room, but more... so much more. "I've always known I want to serve my family, and it's an honor to be invited."

"Ain't like we were brimmin' with options," Pansy replied under her breath.

"There were options," Colleen replied. "I chose you. I chose you because we need the most devout for whatever might lie ahead."

Cassius widened his eyes. Said nothing.

"I won't disappoint you, cousin." He let his eyes fall on the other five. "Or any of you."

There were no further matters to discuss, so Colleen called the meeting adjourned after reminding them that she'd be traveling back to Scotland shortly and would return for quarterly meetings. They took turns embracing her and wishing her well, and then each left, all except Luther.

"Yes, Luther?" Colleen asked as she gathered her folio and pen.

"Can I ask you something?"

"Of course."

"Why *did* you choose me?" Before she could answer, he went on. "Evangeline would've been a clear choice, or even Elizabeth. There are others in the line of Blanche. I know..." He rapped his knuckles against his thighs. "I can't imagine, that is, that you got no pushback, bringing a kid in."

Colleen set her pen inside the folio and pushed it to the side. "Does it matter if I did?"

"I don't know," he said, thinking. He looked around the room filled with portraits of their ancestors. "I just don't want this decision to cause trouble for you."

Colleen scoffed. "I can handle some pushback, Luther. This role wasn't designed to be easy."

"You haven't answered my question."

He was so intense, from his eyes, to his posture. Even his hair, a shocking blond held firmly in place, startled her. Luther Fontenot would be a force one day. "Why you?"

"Yes."

Colleen tilted her head. "You might not like my answer."

"If it's the truth, I'll like it very much."

"Well," Colleen said. "Other than myself, these are your kin on the Council. You know as well as I do, or better, how they think and operate. Don't get me wrong, Luther, they're all very competent, and all care a great deal about the family. But emotional decisions won't carry us through tough times." She understood that saying these things to him, a Fontenot, bore the risk of him carrying the words back to his mother and the others. But Colleen didn't think he'd do that.

"I understand," Luther replied. He shuffled and settled his hands against his torso, looking her square in the eye. "You need an ally."

She couldn't help but laugh. "If you want to put it that way."

"I'm honored to be your ally, Colleen. I've always respected you a great deal, and there aren't many like you... among us. I don't know what's ahead for the family, but if you're looking for pragmatic leadership in challenging times, I won't disappoint you."

She had trouble reminding herself he was only fifteen. Was she so intense at fifteen? So serious? She might've been, especially through the eyes of others.

"That's why I chose you," she said. "Because, like you, I don't know what's ahead for us. But what I do know? Ophelia saw an end to our time of peace. It wasn't like her to give us a warning, but it's coming. I fear for us all if we aren't ready."

Colleen saw Luther out, and then, as she made her way up the stairs, Aria called to her.

"A call came in from Miss Evangeline."

Colleen paused on the stairs and half-turned. "It's way too late in Boston. I'll call her back in the morning."

Aria coughed. "One of her friends was killed. By that... that man hurting women up there. She wanted you to know."

Colleen sagged against the banister. It was past one in New Orleans, an hour later in Boston. But she knew all too well that pain didn't sleep.

"I'll be in my upstairs office," she replied, carrying the unbearable weight of too many things as she ascended once more.

. . .

Nicolas was utterly enchanted by Charles' rudimentary game of peek-a-boo. He'd erupt in fresh giggles with every reveal, as if the previous one hadn't ruined the surprise forever. Each time, his utter delight transported them to a magical place, where there was only innocence and joy. Charles would live there, if he could.

Had his father played these games with him? He had no memory of it, just as Nicolas would have no memory of this. It seemed so unfair, Charles thought, that anything that happened to a person might be beyond the grasp of their memory. Your experiences belonged to you.

Nicolas would be too old for this game soon. He was a year now and already toddling around every room, looking for adventure. He didn't want to lie in his baby rocker, with the dangling toys; he wanted to zoom around, in search of something new to do, to play with, to explore.

In the fall, when the humidity didn't crawl over your skin, Charles would take him outside to play. He couldn't wait to see him explore the roots of the live oaks like a jungle gym, as Charles once had. To run along the maze of gardens flanking the house, squealing as he found a new path, a new bench, a new world to make his own.

But then the door opened.

Darkness crossed the swath of light.

Nicolas' eyes widened, and he looked past Charles now, at whatever had opened the door.

"Mama!" he cried, and Charles' entire world dissolved.

CHAPTER 10

But There is Also Joy

Elizabeth listened to Maureen tell the story of Soren LaViolette with burgeoning surprise.

For once, a story she hadn't seen. But what did that mean, that she'd never experienced glimpses of Maureen and her new, refreshing lover? Would it be so brief as to warrant no vision? Or was there some other reason?

She hoped, listening to Maureen, that it was merely a fluke. Her sister had found her purpose in being a mother, no doubt, but that was not the same thing as seeing her eyes flash and her smile widen so far she had trouble speaking. Maureen as a mother was a thing to behold. Maureen in love was something else entirely.

"And Edouard was completely fine with this?" Elizabeth asked, as she rocked Anasofiya. Nearby, Olivia played with her dolls in an invented language, completely enraptured with whatever storyline her young mind had dreamed up.

"It was his idea!"

Elizabeth shook her head. "Astonishing."

"Lizzy, I *tried* to get him to take more interest in our marriage. When I went to him... that was the outcome I wanted! I wanted him to want me, even if he is an ugly old toad."

"Won't get any disagreement from me. He *is* an ugly old toad, and he's no match for your sexual needs, that's for sure."

"Trust me, he has his own needs," Maureen said with a strange look. "They just die once he's done chasing someone. For someone like that, what could be worse than a wife?"

"But, through you, he has Olivia." *And someday, a son.*

Maureen nodded slowly, sipping her lemonade. Augustus, of all people, had made it. He was full of strange surprises now that he was home all the time. At present, he was gardening in the back with Connor. He'd tried to take Ana, but Elizabeth talked him out of it by reminding him the sweltering humidity was no place for a little one. She did a lot of that now, searching for counterarguments that appealed to his fears. It was often the only way to get him to take care of himself, too.

"He does, and I think he's growing fond of her," Maureen said. "She won't want for anything material, ever. But I worry... that when she's older, she'll see our façade of a marriage and know that she lives under the same illusion. You know?"

"She has you. And us," Elizabeth said. "And Edouard might surprise you."

"I hope he does," Maureen said. She chewed her bottom lip. "Soren has."

"I can see that."

Maureen lowered her voice, as if either child had any comprehension of the conversation. "We haven't even had *sex* yet, Lizzy."

"That must be hard for you."

"No! That's the thing! It's not hard at all... it's... it's..."

"Weird to like a guy for more than his dick?"

"Shh!"

"They're babies, Maureen. Not so easily scandalized."

"Still." Maureen shook her head. "What's weird is, I don't even *care* if we do have sex. And the whole point of taking a lover was to satisfy my needs."

"You are satisfying your needs," Elizabeth replied. "Maybe they're just needs you didn't know you had."

Maureen tilted her head to the side. It was clear this hadn't ever occurred to her, that her needs might go beyond the base, feral desire for sex. Elizabeth was suddenly very sad. They were all so damaged, in their own ways, but Maureen had suffered especially.

"I don't know," Maureen said slowly. "Even if you're right, what good is that to me? I can't ever have a normal relationship with Soren."

Elizabeth snorted. "When has *anything* about being a Deschanel ever been normal?"

"You know what I mean."

Elizabeth shrugged. She shifted a sleeping Ana to her other shoulder, carefully, to avoid waking her. "A lot of women have lovers, Maureen. Not all get their husband's permission."

"But what if Soren one day wants more? More than I can give?"

"You're getting ahead of yourself."

Maureen's eyes narrowed. "Have you seen my future? Do you know?"

"I wouldn't break my rule to tell you," Elizabeth said. "But I haven't seen anything at all. It's rare for me to be surprised, but I am today."

Maureen drew blood on her lip with her chewing. "But maybe that means... maybe that means there *is* no future for us, that I'm getting worked up about nothing, and—"

"Stop," Elizabeth said. "I haven't seen anything from Charles, either, or Colleen, or Evie. I think it's because I spend all my time here. All I see are images from Augustus, or Ana."

Maureen leaned in. "You've seen her future?" She traced her fingers gently over Ana's fine red hair. "Does Augustus know?"

"Does Augustus know *what*?" He appeared in the doorway, sweat mixed with dirt in his pores, cleaning his hands with a rag.

Maureen pulled her jaw tight as if to say, *oops.*

Elizabeth liked to think her rule was steadfast, but she'd already broken it for her brother once before. As with the last time, the thought plagued her that telling him might save him from himself.

"I, uh..." Elizabeth exhaled. "I've seen glimpses of Ana's future."

Augustus froze. His expression darkened. "No..."

She shook her head wildly. "Aggie, it's not what you think. It's..." She drew in a hard breath. "Like all of us, Ana will have hardships, but she'll also have joy. She won't end up like her mother."

"You're breaking your rule."

"Twice, for you, and only you, but who's counting?"

Augustus' mouth parted. He reached to his side to grip the doorframe. "You wouldn't lie to me?"

"Never about this." She glanced at Maureen and then stood, taking Ana with her. She slipped the little one into her father's arms. "Look at her. Don't be afraid."

Augustus' lower lip quavered as he first cast his eyes across the room, and then, fluttering, trained them on his daughter.

"The dark cloud following you ends with her. She has a darkness, too, but the light is bigger." Elizabeth touched his cheek. "You're the light, Augustus."

FALL 1976

NEW ORLEANS, LOUISIANA
VACHERIE, LOUISIANA
CAMBRIDGE, MASSACHUSETTS
EDINBURGH, SCOTLAND

CHAPTER 11

Worst Kept Secret

Robyn Sullivan was a beautiful baby. Colleen thought most babies were beautiful, especially in the glow of their mother's arms, but Robyn had a special radiance about her, as if she was given something a little extra to make up for her inauspicious entrance into the world.

But although she would not be raised by either her birth mother or father, Robyn would never know anything but unconditional love. To see the small family, an outsider looking in, one would never know Robyn wasn't anything more or less than the daughter Carolina so desperately wanted. Their miracle baby, they called her, in the birth announcements, and from the damp twinkle in Carolina's eyes anytime she looked at Robyn, this was undoubtedly true.

Rory's worries melted into wonder as he held his baby daughter. If he still had doubts, he didn't put them into words.

Their family was complete.

While Noah made conversation with the happy new parents, Amelia sleeping soundly in his arms, Colleen slipped away to the bedroom where Catherine stayed throughout her confinement. She found the new mother packing her small suitcase, hunched over the bed with the weight of weariness spread over and through her. Three weeks had passed since Robyn's birth. It was time for her to leave and let Robyn be loved by her forever family now.

"I haven't thanked you properly, Colleen," Catherine said, without turning her head. She tossed her clothes in haphazardly, without a care for neatness or organization. A hairbrush lay akimbo atop skirts, skirts atop tubes of mascara. A can of hair-spray nested between clothes.

"How did you know it was me?"

"They can't even look at me," Catherine said with a laugh. "It's as if they think I'll change my mind and take my baby back. *Their* baby." She tossed her feathered hair, jagged and dry from lack of care, and her laugh turned darker. "As if I lived in a world where that was possible."

"That may not be possible, but your happiness is," Colleen said carefully.

"Is it?"

"Only you can find it for yourself."

Catherine ripped at the zipper on her bag, her movements clipped, angry. "What do you want me to say?"

"I want you to be okay," Colleen replied. She'd never been especially close to Catherine and never approved of her behavior with Charles, but there was a deep sadness about Catherine that made it hard to ever really want to see the young woman suffer for her errant and indecisive recklessness.

"I've never been okay," Catherine said. "I'll never *be* okay."

"What will you do?"

"Go home."

"To Colin."

"Yes, Colleen. Where else would I go?"

"Your life doesn't have to be a series of things you think you should do. Have you thought about what you *want* to do?"

"I wanted Charles."

Colleen tensed. She didn't want to upset Catherine further,

but this line of conversation was infuriating. She *could've* had Charles, but chose stability over passion. Catherine's life was a series of misguided choices, each one focused on self-preservation, no matter the cost to herself or others. "That ship has sailed."

"You don't think I know that? I hear he's moved on, anyway. To his fucking *maid*, of all things."

"His marriage is unhappy. Something I know you understand."

"And now she's pregnant, but unlike me, she'll get to keep her baby. Her Deschanel bastard."

Colleen winced. News traveled fast. "She is, and yes, Charles intends to keep her there and raise the child with Nicolas. But if you're thinking these two situations are *at all* the same—"

Catherine spun around. "I'm not an idiot, Colleen."

"I never said—"

"I know you want this whole thing tied in a neat little bow so you can go back to Scotland completely pleased with yourself—"

It was Colleen's turn to shut the other woman down. "That's not the least bit fair, or right. *You* came to *me*, and if you think this 'little thing' was on my list of stuff to deal with, after losing my aunt, my sister-in-law, my whole *world* breaking down, then you should step outside your self-centered world, for even a second, and look around at what's happening. But I rose to the occasion, because it was the right thing to do, not just for you, but for Charles. For Colin, who's my lifelong friend, and whose family is an extension of mine. For your daughter, who deserves better than to be the catalyst that rips both our families apart. And never forget, it wasn't my decision to have an affair that produced a child you didn't know what to do with. Nor was it my decision for you to give her up, Catherine, and if you would start, for once in your life, *owning* your own actions, you might understand how fortunate you are that this situation had an outcome that left your daughter cared for and your marriage intact. It isn't for me to judge you, and I won't, but I'll be damned if I keep watching you blow through Charles' life like a hurricane without direction and then weep like you're the only one damaged. You don't get to burn the house down and then cry over the ashes. At least not with me."

Colleen didn't wait for Catherine's response. She left her alone with the remnants of a dying fantasy of another world.

"A NANNY," CORDELIA REPEATED. "FOR OUR... NANNY."

"Saying it like a condescending bitch doesn't add clarity to the situation," Charles said, through clenched teeth, cigarette bobbing. He'd been under the hood of his TransAm for over an hour, and his frustration mounted by the second at things not being more intuitive. The more he thought about how fucking ridiculous that notion was, that he'd open the hood and the answers would appear, as if by magic, the deeper his irrational anger took root and bloomed into a more colorful rage. How was he supposed to run a household if he couldn't even find the oil pan?

Just not the same as my old TransAm that got destroyed on our wedding day when God rained down his disapproval. That's all.

But it was, and he knew it was, and he wanted to knock the beast off its blocks and send it careening into the swamp for the audacity to present him with a challenge when he already had so much on his mind.

A girl, but you knew that, too, didn't you? Elizabeth said, as she slid into the passenger seat yesterday, of a car driven by Connor. As if that strange little vision wasn't enough—his baby sister, her boyfriend, in a goddamn *car*, without adults because they *were* the goddamn adults—she managed to elicit an emotional response he thought he'd buried forever when he destroyed the envelope that carried the location of his only daughter.

"This isn't a circus, Charles. That whore carrying your children, while pretending to raise our son, is the worst kept secret in New Orleans. You wanted me to stay so people wouldn't talk, but if you hire a nanny for the woman hired to raise our son, you—wait, are you *smoking* under the hood of a car?"

"I let you stay because you're penniless and I'm not a complete piece of shit." Charles inhaled a lungful of smoke and blew it out his nose. "When you're done training to become a mechanic, come talk to me about fucking cars."

"You've been out here for two hours. Trying to change your oil."

"The issue is more complex than that," he muttered. "You wouldn't understand."

"Is it, though?"

"I can't begin to explain it to you."

"You told Lisette you came to change your oil."

Charles grumbled and stubbed out his smoke.

Cordelia uncrossed her arms and pointed. "You haven't even drained the oil. The drain plug is right"—Cordelia leaned in and tapped on the side of the engine—"here." She looked around, brows furrowing tighter with every discovery. "Oh dear. You don't even have a pan to catch the oil. And where's the new oil filter?"

Charles considered, for at least the seven-hundredth time, how much smoother his life would be if he murdered his wife. But no one had a greater motive than he did, and he didn't think he could ever look Nicolas in the eye again.

He wasn't looking his son in the eye much anymore anyway, not since Lisette's pregnancy news, but that was another matter, one he didn't have the emotional fortitude to unpack and properly address. Not while the matter of his oil change remained unsolved.

Mama.

Charles had been at the center of Nicolas' world his whole life, and Cordelia comes back for a week and all that is forgotten.

Mama.

"Charles? Did you want help with this?"

"What do you know about oil changes, anyway?" he said, sneering. "Of course I know where the plug is."

"My father's hobby was working on old cars," Cordelia said. She scooted in and nudged him out of the way. "Grab me a couple of pans off the shelf and..." She frowned. "I know Richard has oil filters for you, because I've seen them. Can you check with him?"

Charles' mouth flapped in astonishment, but he put one foot in front of the other and made his way back to the Big House to do as she asked.

Was he growing soft?

No, he decided, he just had limits, same as any man, and fighting with her wasn't in the cards today.

When he returned, Cordelia had hitched her dress into a knot at her side, sleeves pulled up, hair held back with her reading glasses. Her arms were buried under the hood to the elbows, and then she slid down, on her back and under the car, held aloft by ramps, scraping the pans under where she'd loosened the plug.

Sometimes—and this was one of those times—he realized he didn't know his wife at all.

"Filter?"

"Huh? Oh. Yeah." Charles knelt and placed it in her impatiently waving hand.

"It still needs to drain a bit, but easier to keep it nearby, so we don't lose it." She extracted herself from under the car. She was covered in oil, her dress ruined. Sepia smudges stained her cheeks. He resisted the urge to wipe them away; pushed aside the errant notion that she was, sometimes, actually quite pretty.

Until she opened her mouth.

"Thanks," he grumbled.

"What was that?"

"I said *thanks*," he said, louder, but strained.

"Next time, just hire a mechanic," she said, blowing a stray hair out of her dirty face. "Of all the things to be cheap about, I swear, Charles."

"I wasn't being cheap," he defended. *I just wanted to feel like one of those salt-of-the-earth men, just for a little while.*

"Anyway," Cordelia said, wiping her hands on a shop towel he hadn't seen her pull out. "Give that a good fifteen, twenty minutes to drain. It's muddy because you haven't changed it in way too long. You're lucky the damn engine hasn't exploded. If you still need my help, when it comes time to swap out the filter, call... a mechanic," she finished, with a hard look that made him think, *ahh, welcome back, there you are.*

"I can do it," he insisted, but he'd wait until she was gone into town to call his mechanic.

"Sure," she replied, and he wanted to slap the subsequent look from her face. "About the nanny."

"Look, it was my idea, not hers."

"Oh, I know," Cordelia said, her smile growing from the corner of her mouth. "Lisette wasn't born looking for others to do things for her. If I had to guess, I'd say you're fighting about this. Am I right? Is this a sore spot between you two?"

It was, but he wouldn't give her the pleasure. "She wants to raise her own kid. Who am I to stop her?"

"Spoken like a true man."

"What's that supposed to mean?"

"Nothing, only I can't wait to see the medals she gives you for changing diapers, taking the baby for a spin in the stroller, and the occasional game of peek-a-boo."

"Spoken like a woman who's missed half her son's life while she was off having never-ending spa days with the women her father paid to be her friend."

"Remind me again, Charles," she said, turning halfway to the house for her final twist of the knife. "What was Nicolas' first word?"

"Cambridge suits you," Colleen remarked with a smile after Evangeline sat back down in her seat at the outdoor café along Boston Common.

"This is a nice surprise," Evangeline said, but she looked more wary than anything else. "Doesn't your flight to Edinburgh pass through New York?"

"Just as easy to go through Boston, turns out."

"Where are Noah and Amelia?"

"Oh, Noah took her to explore some Revolutionary war ship in the harbor," Colleen said with a flip of her hand. "He's a bit of a war historian, I'm learning. He was very excited about seeing all the founding father memorabilia and telling Amelia about it, even if she won't remember a thing."

"I'd like to have met her, you know."

Colleen's face turned immediately stricken. "Evie, I completely forgot you hadn't. My mind is all over the place these days. Maybe we can meet them at the harbor after lunch?"

"How long are you here?"

"We leave tomorrow."

Evangeline's eyes narrowed. "When did you get in?"

"Yesterday."

"Short trip."

"Is this an interrogation?"

"Just seems weird. That's all. No notice. You just show up..."

"Weird that I want to see my sister?"

"Without calling? Out of the blue? Spontaneously? Yes."

Colleen wrung her hands under the table. She hated to lie, under any circumstance, but especially to Evie. The strength of their bond relied on the purest form of honesty; the rawest of vulnerabilities.

But this isn't your truth, Colleen.

"I realized that I might not see you again until Christmas."

"And that's if I come home," Evangeline said, tearing off a hunk of bread from the basket the waiter dropped off. She shoved it in her mouth and continued. "I only came home last Christmas because everything at home was a mess."

"Who says it's not a mess still?"

Evangeline swallowed and tore off more bread. "You're going back to Scotland, so it must have settled some."

"My life is there now. With Noah and Amelia."

"You stayed in New Orleans for six months, Leena."

Colleen refused a drink, opting for water. Evangeline ignored the waiter altogether, until he walked away with an awkward shuffle. "Is that an accusation, or a question?"

"Just making a point."

"Okay," Colleen said, drawing out her syllables. "There were a few reasons, I suppose. I had work to do, to set things up in Ophelia's absence. I was worried our brother was going off the deep end, and since you haven't asked, I'll just say this: he's wearing denim. Yes, Augustus. Take that as you will. I didn't think Amelia would be ready for an airplane in her first few months, and I wanted her to have time with Mama and her uncles and aunts before I took her away again."

"Those are all good reasons," Evangeline said, her face unreadable.

"But?"

"But that doesn't explain why you're here. And why you look so..."

"So, what?"

"I don't know. Jittery."

Colleen tensed. "Well, Evie, it's been a jittery few months for us."

"No," Evangeline said, wagging her finger. "That's not it."

"I don't know what you're getting at. I just wanted to see my sister."

"Okay, Colleen," Evangeline said and a sudden smile spread over her face. "Whatever your reasons, I'm glad you're here."

"Whatever my—" Colleen shook her head. "Tell me about you. Last time we talked, when you called..."

"Yeah," Evangeline said. "You said I should take my power back. So I did."

Colleen folded her hands and leaned in. She took a drink from her water. "Tell me about it."

Evangeline's smile widened. "I'm learning kung-fu and I bought a gun."

Colleen nearly spat her mouthful of water across the table. "You *what*?"

"I'm learning kung-fu and I bought a gun."

"Why on earth would you buy a gun?"

Evangeline twisted her mouth into a near pout. "You're the one who said to take my power back."

"We apparently have a very different idea of what that means!"

"Why are you giving me a hard time?"

"Well." Colleen pushed her water out of the way. "For starters, statistically, you're more likely to have that gun turned on you in an altercation than you are to defend yourself in one."

"Yes, my friend Ian, the statistics major, pointed that out as well."

"Okay, and how about this: you've never fired a gun in your life?"

"Not yet."

"What does that mean? Not yet? You waiting until you're in an actual life and death situation?"

"No."

"What am I missing? If you were sitting where I'm at, you'd be giving the same lecture, and probably be doing a better job at it," Colleen said.

"Well, Leena, I might've prepared better if I'd known you were coming before, oh, *yesterday*."

Colleen, in an abrupt rush of instinct, reached across the table and gripped Evangeline's hands in hers. "I don't like this, Evie. *This*, whatever it is, happening right now. Between us."

Evangeline lowered her head. "I don't either."

"You think I'm acting strange, and I think you're making strange decisions," Colleen said. "But I just *miss* you. I miss us."

"Yeah," Evangeline said, lifting her gaze. Her eyes glistened. "I do too."

"So instead of fighting, why don't we go walk through the Common, and you can show me this place that's changed your life."

Evangeline smiled. "Don't lose sleep over me owning a gun, Leena. I'm going to learn to use it, and I'm going to practice, and keep doing that, until it's no longer this *thing*, but an extension of me, and a twitch on the thread of my instincts."

CHAPTER 12

Dada

D*ada. Dada.*
Dada.
Dada.

Nicolas toddled around behind him, from room to room, practically screaming the word. The word should have been a salve, but instead it was something else, like napalm, but even more explosive. Dangerous.

For him. For Nicolas.

Because, *Mama.* Mama was first. Mama, the only word on earth capable of driving a wedge between him and his impenetrable love for Nicolas. What he *thought* was impenetrable love, but had been undone with a single word, and then buried deeper into the ground with another word, the one he craved all along and now was the ignition switch.

"Not now," he grumbled as the beautiful boy, head full of dark hair and eyes like his father's bounced around behind him, not understanding; his mood first curious and light, but the longer Charles ignored him, the more desperate his *dadas* grew; the more strained, laced with the terror of not understanding.

This is your fault. You fucking hellbeast. You abominable witch.

This continued, with Charles' heart beating hard enough to

cause black spots to push at the back of his eyeballs, Nicolas' anguished cries carving scars into both of them, until Lisette appeared and swept him up into her arms.

"My sweet baby boy," Lisette cooed into Nicolas' red, damp face. She pressed her lips into his hair and shot Charles a chilling look across the hall. "Let's go get snack, Nicky," she said, eyes never leaving the father, who had failed at this, as he failed at everything.

I'm sorry.

"Is this how you be with daughter, too?" Lisette accused as she brushed by him, Nicolas sobbing in her arms.

"No," Charles replied weakly, and there was no point in explaining why that would be different, because they both knew, and the answer didn't exonerate him. The answer didn't bring back his love, nor did it kill his resentment. The answer was as pointless as love, as pointless as joy, which was dependent upon conditions that never lasted.

He would love his daughter until circumstances prevented him, and then he'd find something else to love. Something equally transient, and equally, exquisitely painful when it was time to release it.

Maureen rode the rise and fall of Soren's bony chest. She always wriggled to find a place to nestle in, but Soren neither had the flab of her middle school teacher, or the taut lines of the high school boys. His body was merely a vessel for other things, and he gave it as much, or as little, disregard as it required in the moment.

The sex was amazing. She expected no less, but what she *hadn't* expected was that it was this, these moments or hours afterward, that she craved far more. Sometimes, when they were a tangle of sweat and moans, her mind would drift into the future, where she knew these tender interludes awaited. Where they would talk about everything, and nothing, and sometimes there wasn't anything to say, just emotions traveling through their tired flesh, mingling into a single sensation.

Maureen was *not* a romantic. She liked to say, to herself, to Chelsea, to anyone who'd listen, that she was too practical for romance. Her needs were more fundamental, like that triangle—no, pyramid, she was pretty sure it was a pyramid—they learned about in health class, the one that talked about how you had no goddamn use for the fancy shit until your basic needs, like a house, like food, like security, were met. She said as much to her mother once, who laughed, and said, what would a rich girl know about it? But a rich girl could know just as much disappointment, as much pain, as much heartache, as a poor girl. A rich girl could learn to live with what she had, whatever that might be, and never want for more.

"Paris," Soren said, answering his own question. "What about you?"

"I've never really thought about it," Maureen said. Her fingers slayed across his soft, lean belly. What did they even call this? The sex Maureen had had was over as soon as the man came, and then they returned to their own lives. They never lingered... talked.

Soren removed one hand from behind his head and brushed Maureen's face aside, so he could see it. "You've never thought about leaving New Orleans? Not once? Never considered starting over?"

"I didn't say that, I just never thought about where I might go."

"So think about it now."

His words, soft and inviting, rather than forceful, inspired her to do just that. "I've never really been anywhere."

"How's that possible?"

"When my father died, we stopped doing things as a family," Maureen said. "I was just a kid. He always talked about going to Europe, or Africa, like he did as a boy, but then he was gone, and Mama only had use for the essentials."

Soren ran her hair through his fingers. "Is there anywhere you'd like to go?"

"London," she said, without hesitation, realizing that was also the answer to the first question, though she'd never been there. "Or Kent."

"Why London?"

"My favorite book is set there."

"Wait, don't tell me. I want to guess." Soren's hand stopped moving, and she could hear him thinking; could feel his soft smile. "*Great Expectations.*"

Maureen jumped up onto one elbow. "How did you...?"

"You remind me a little bit of Estella," he replied, but quickly added, "the best of her, that is. She wasn't all bad. She was made that way."

"You don't think Estella chose to be a self-centered bitch?"

"It was the path of least resistance. That's what most people take."

"That's very..."

"Nihilistic?" Soren finished. He settled back into his pillow and resumed his sweet, mindless playing of Maureen's hair. "I don't know. I'm more of a realist, and I know better than to expect more than what someone's nature or environment has built them to be. I do love when people surprise me, though." He kissed the top of her tangled hair. "You surprised me."

"How so?"

"I thought you were a bored Garden District housewife who wouldn't have anything interesting to say."

Maureen stopped breathing for a moment. "And..."

"You actually have something to say."

Maureen couldn't recall ever saying anything especially important to Soren, so she waited for him to explain.

"We all survive this world in different ways, Maureen. Some of us choose the path of least resistance, and others fight uphill, against the snow, the rain, the wind, the earth itself. Your life isn't easy. I like to say mine isn't, but really, how bad can it be, living off the salt of my family, in this beautiful estate, writing poetry?"

"But you can't live the life you most want."

"Meanwhile, there are children in Africa who haven't had dinner for a week."

Maureen frowned against his skin. "Yes, but... is it really fair to compare your life to something that has nothing to do with you? Isn't your disappointment still disappointment? Children can starve, you can be unfulfilled. One doesn't cancel out the other."

"Still surprising me," Soren said lightly. "I can't argue with that. There are more ways than one to look at the world. I like people who remind me of that."

"And I do?"

Soren laced his arms around her and pulled her up to kiss her. With one hand, he held her hair off her forehead, and his eyes burned a hole through her. A perfect, delicious hole that he'd soon fill with more of him. "You remind me to remember. I'd lost some of my hope before I met you, and... I have to admit to you, when I agreed to meet, it wasn't because I had any notion of finding someone I might like. I needed an escape, same as you, and instead I found..."

"Something else," Maureen finished, not quite sure if it *was* right, or only felt right.

"Yeah," Soren said, with a gentle, faraway look, as he kissed her again. "Something else."

"Congratulations," Augustus said. "And thanks for coming to meet me."

"You're being weird again," Charles said, wrinkling his lips as he downed a tumbler of cognac. He waved the glass around in front of him, in Augustus' direction. "And what is this? You're wearing a jean jacket? Where in the sweet fuck did you get that? Did you steal it from Connor?"

Augustus looked down and held the flaps of his denim with a confused look. “This isn’t in fashion?”

“Jesus on a hominy grit, Aggie, of course it is, but when have *you* ever cared about fashion?”

Augustus recoiled a bit. “I’m not working right now, so it hardly seemed appropriate to wear my Brooks Brothers.”

“I always assumed you slept in the shit.”

“Funny.”

“Not as funny as you looking like you’re one step away from asking me to call you Pony Boy.”

“*The Outsiders* is a great book. You know, Charles, books, where there are words, and pages, and—”

“Ha-fucking-ha. Okay, I deserved that.” Charles held up two fingers to the bartender, who should know better by now than to set only one glass in front of him. “How long is this, er, hiatus from work going to last anyway?”

“I don’t know. As long as it needs to.”

“I see.”

“If you did, you wouldn’t be asking.” Augustus checked his Rolex. “I told Elizabeth I’d be home in an hour, so I suppose I’ll get to the point.”

“You think she’s gonna boil Ana in a stew or something if you’re late?” Charles nodded at the bartender, who brought not two, but three more. *Atta boy.* “Don’t forget, Lizzy can’t cook.”

Augustus glared. “I’m here about Nicolas.”

“What about him?”

“I know you’ve gone cold toward him, and I want to know why.”

“You know something, do you?” Charles pushed his empty glasses to the side. “Who the fuck have you been talking to?”

“Mama told me.”

“What the fuck does Mama know about the price of tea in China?”

Augustus shook his head, apparently deciding not to try to unwind the weird things his brother said. “Mama heard it from

Lisette's mother, who presumably heard it from her. But does it matter who told who? Is it true?"

Charles snorted and swished the cognac around in the glass. He looked away.

"Charles." Augustus laid a hand on his shoulder. "Huck."

"I don't want to talk about it."

"Did something happen?"

Mama. Mama. Mama. "I said I don't want to talk about it."

"He's your *son*," Augustus said. "He's just a baby, Huck. There's nothing he could've done to cause this, and so it must be something else."

"Why do you care?"

"I care, and I know you care, too. For once in your life, you have a reason to care."

"You don't know as much as you think you do, Augustus."

Augustus wrapped his palm around Charles' forearm. "Do you remember what you said to me, when Ana was born? When you came into the room and made me promise?"

"People say bullshit all the time."

"You meant it," Augustus said. "I've never seen you mean something more. Ever. I've never seen you care about anything, or anyone, with the intensity you care about your son."

"Don't take the shit I say on a whim as gospel, Aggie. I fall in and out of love all the time. Remember when I thought I was in love with Cat?"

"You *are* in love with Cat," Augustus corrected. "It just didn't work out."

"Pfft. I couldn't care less about the bitch anymore."

"I didn't come to talk about Cat."

Charles rolled his wrist forward in a dramatic check of the Rolex whose battery had stopped years ago. "Isn't your daughter at risk of being boiled alive?"

Augustus pressed his lips tight. "Fine. You don't want to talk about it, I can't make you. But I'm sending Connor out to pick Nicolas up to stay with us for a few days. Until you can... I don't know, work out whatever's gotten into you. Until you're ready to be a dad again. He shouldn't suffer while you figure yourself out."

"Great. Come get him," Charles said, throwing a bill down on the bar. "But don't hold your breath about the last part. It's like that with me, you know. Everything has an end. Sometimes it just comes sooner than you hope."

Augustus sighed as Charles put his wallet back in his pocket. "The promise meant something to me, anyway."

CHAPTER 13

Crazy is Relative

Augustus loved having Nicolas in his household.

It was good for Ana, to have another little one around to make fake conversations with, but it was good for him, as well. Augustus wouldn't have figured himself for a baby person and was pleasantly surprised that his enjoyment of them wasn't limited to the one he'd fathered.

He had half a mind to call up Maureen, tell her to send Olivia for a couple weeks as well, but they all thought he was crazy, and a request like that wouldn't go very far toward correcting that belief.

Was he crazy?

Augustus had spent considerable time ruminating over this very question. Sometimes it took him to dark places, others it assuaged him. But his only strong conclusion, no matter which road he turned down, was that crazy was relative. Craziness was a wheel, like time, and depending on where you were, in relation to others, to different places, circumstances, the result of that question varied considerably. Then he'd laugh when he realized "crazy is relative," could be so easily translated to "crazy is a relative," because *ha-ha-ha* family *did* drive you crazy!

Of course, when you laughed at your own words, which weren't so much funny as ironic, you found yourself on a part of the wheel you might consider quickly exiting.

Grief was a path to madness. That he did understand, both objectively and how he was now, sunken in the mud keeping him from advancing to the next stage of the process. Evangeline had explained to him, clearly believing science was the only way to dredge him from the recesses of suffering, that a Swiss-American psychiatrist had recently come up with something called the Kübler-Ross model, which explained that grief was a seven-stage cycle. He'd moved quickly from the shock and denial phase into guilt, but he also, sometimes felt anger, which was supposed to come next, but seeped into his everyday tasks. And then there were days where he thought he'd imagined it all and slipped back into denial. Then there were days the depression swallowed him whole, which was supposed to be farther down the list, and others where he thought he was pulling out of it altogether. He experienced all seven stages, sometimes in the same day, so Augustus wasn't so sure about this new-fangled philosophy on grief.

But most of the time, it was guilt. Guilt that his sadness of losing Ekatherina had faded more quickly than any hurt of his life thus far. Guilt that he was, sometimes, even relieved she was gone. Guilt that he'd prioritized the life of their child over her. Guilt that he struggled to understand her, but truly could've tried harder, had he really wanted to. Guilt that she was, somehow, another Maddy. Another failure of his inability to be human.

Guilt that the child he'd do anything for, that he'd *die* for, was stuck with him.

Earlier that day, he'd overheard Elizabeth talking to Connor.

"Both my brothers are descending into madness," she'd said. "Only different kinds."

As Augustus watched Nicolas playing with Anasofiya, he thought to himself that he'd take his madness over his brother's any day.

. . .

"WHAT DO YOU *MEAN* YOU SENT OUR SON TO YOUR brother's?"

"You repeated it, so you heard it." Charles rifled through the pantry, searching for where he'd hidden the Goldfish crackers. If he didn't hide them, Lisette would eat them, and while he didn't mind indulging her pregnant whims, this was the one thing off-limits.

"I heard what you said. What I'm struggling with is what you intended by it."

"I *intended* to take Augustus up on his offer to take Nicolas."

"For how long?"

"However long he wants him."

"Charles."

Charles slammed his hand against the shelf. "Cordelia."

"As with many things in your life, you've lost interest in our son. It's tragic, but not shocking, given your history," Cordelia said. "But I have *not* lost interest. It might surprise you to know I'm actually quite fond of him."

"Fond." Charles snorted. "As if you were talking about snack food."

"*I* ate the last of your Goldfish. Your hiding places are predictable. Will you get a grip?" Cordelia replied with a whiff of exasperation. "Call Augustus. I want Nicolas back here by tonight."

"Call him yourself."

"I'll do no such thing. You started this mess. You fix it."

"What mess?"

"Going cold on our son."

"I haven't gone cold on him."

"What started it?" Cordelia put a hand on his arm. Her tone had softened. "Seriously, Charles. It's just us here. Tell me."

Charles shrugged off her icy touch and started to launch into a tirade of barbs and curse words, but something stopped him. Why not tell her? So what if it gave her power? So what? She had so little, and he could take away whatever she did possess with a snap of his fingers.

"You abandoned him at birth, and you come back and his first fucking word is *Mama.*"

Cordelia's face shifted swiftly from kindness to amusement. Her lips played with her choice of words. Then, she started laughing.

"What's so fucking funny?"

"Oh, Charles." She doubled over, cackling. "You silly, petty man."

Charles' rage burst through from his toes, radiating throughout him in a split second. He barged past her, past her laughter, her coldness, her utter horribleness as a human being.

"His first words weren't *Mama*, you brute. You absolute idiot," she called after him. "He came back from that silly parade crying out *Dada* like a broken record! Waving those beads around, so proud to have something to give *Dada*!"

Charles rage turned to ice. He froze, his breath trapped in his chest.

"Look at you, a grown man treating your toddler son like he committed a criminal act, for a crime he didn't even commit!"

"You keep pulling your support-side leg back and straightening your strong-side foot," Joshua said. He was cradled behind her, working to correct her stance. He'd already adjusted her arms and hands, helping her find the right tension between the support hand and the strong hand. Even with her appreciation of physics, Evangeline was surprised at how important small adjustments were to both her control and precision.

Cassie was a natural. Joshua nudged her elbows once or twice, but other than that, he watched her with a surprised sort of pride as she fired off an entire clip like she'd been doing it her whole life.

"You wanna tell me something?" Evangeline teased. "You one of those girls on that show that just came out?"

"*Charlie's Angels*?" Cassie asked, as she switched out her clip. Her ear protection lay at her neck.

"See, you guessed on the first try, so you already know you're a bad motherfucker."

"My father is a cop." Cassie slid the earphones back on and squared her stance.

A cop. Cassie was Evangeline's best friend, but this fact was new to her, as so many were. Cassie talked a lot but said so little about herself.

"Ready to try again?" Joshua asked, dropping back in behind Evangeline. "There you go. Legs look great. Just bend the support side elbow a touch, and... yes, that's it. Perfect." He slid her ear protection up over her head and backed away.

The next shots felt good. No, they felt great. The power transferred from the trunk of her body, but it started somewhere deeper, somewhere dark and damaged, and as she did so, she let more of the light in.

Evangeline kept firing until it was only clicks. She looked at the gun, confused at how she'd gone through an entire clip in what felt like seconds. That's when she noticed both Cassie and Joshua were staring at her.

He pressed a button and the target rolled toward them. "Were you hustling us, or what?" Joshua asked, only half-joking.

Evangeline saw the results of her practice for the first time. It shouldn't have been for the first time, but she'd gone somewhere else as the firepower coursed through her. She'd become someone else.

Cassie whistled. The air had gone out of their corner of the room. "Jesus, Evie. You sure you're not one of Charlie's angels?"

"I don't know what happened." Evangeline lowered the gun. She removed the clip and set both on the towel Joshua had provided. "I don't know how I did that."

"Maybe that's enough for today," Joshua said, reaching carefully past her. He inspected the chamber and then backed away. "Same time tomorrow?"

At the bus stop, Cassie turned to Evangeline. "You know, it's good for us to feel safe. But we'd feel safer, I think, if we didn't go home alone every night."

"What do you mean?" Evangeline was only half-listening. She struggled to piece together the memories of the fugue state in the firing range.

"I mean, why don't we move in together?"

"Roommates?"

"Yeah, for now. Until they catch the killer."

Evangeline hadn't considered this, but wished she had, and much sooner. Cassie was the one person who didn't belittle her fears, or chastise her for buying a gun. She seemed to understand, maybe because she was the same, or maybe not, but the reasons didn't matter.

She linked arms with her friend. "Let's do it."

AUGUSTUS DROPPED THE MAIL PILE ON THE SILVER tray. Nicolas gripped his pant legs. Anasofiya, strapped to his back, cooed and pointed at the most colorful piece of mail, at the top of the stack.

The fall edition of Deschanel Magazine.

For the first time, Augustus didn't know what he'd find inside. He was afraid to open it; to witness something he couldn't recognize, something no longer his.

But he didn't have time to think about this, because Elizabeth burst through the door, eyes wide, cheeks flushed with panic.

"Hurricane Francine," she panted.

"What about it?" It was supposed to miss them entirely and just nick the southern end of Texas. The seventh storm of the season, and all had been uneventful.

His mother's words jumped into his head. She said them, in some form, every year, and the last time was at Patrick Sullivan's wedding. *We're due for another big one, you know. Betsy, in '65, was bad, but it's been many years since we've seen utter disaster.*

"It turned."

Augustus tensed. "What do you mean it turned?"

"The weather team is saying it's turned and now it's going to hit New Orleans," Connor said, appearing behind Elizabeth. He nearly crashed into her.

"No, that's not... when?"

"Too soon for us to evacuate," Connor replied. He scanned the room with nervous eyes.

"How is that possible, though?" Augustus reached behind him and lifted Ana from her carrier, and cradled her against his chest. "How did we miss the evacuation orders?"

"We didn't," Elizabeth said. "Because they never gave them."

"I don't understand."

"The governor was on television just now, Augustus. They aren't saying, but sounds like someone was asleep on the job, or they didn't get the news out quick enough. They're advising against evacuation because when Francine hits everyone will be stuck on I-10, and that would be... well, a disaster. They're going to sound the emergency system soon, and then everyone should be indoors, with their hurricane kits. Storm shutters bolted. How's the attic here?"

Augustus was too dazed to answer. A hurricane? He wasn't ready for this. Not when Ana... when Nicolas...

"Augustus? You do have a hurricane kit, right?"

"What? Yes. Yeah, it's in the pantry."

"I'll go get it." Connor exchanged a look with Elizabeth. "It's too late to send your housekeeper home, so she's staying. We're all staying. Lizzy, get some blankets to the attic, and I'll start taking supplies up. See if Beatrice can help, since she's staying. And, uh... I don't know, as much water as you can take, I suppose."

"The cradles," Augustus managed. "For the babies."

Connor gripped his arm. "Don't worry about a thing, Aggie. Lizzy and I got this. Just keep the babies safe, and we'll be ready when this thing hits us."

"Mama," Augustus managed, shouting after Elizabeth. "Someone has to go get her! She can't be alone in this."

Elizabeth reached for the keys and threw them at Connor. "Go!"

CHAPTER 14
It Wasn't Supposed to Turn

Maureen was greeted at Soren's country manor with a face full of raw panic.

"Maureen, what are you *doing* here?" He raced behind her and shut the door, bolting all three locks. "I've been calling you for the past hour."

"You called my house?" Maureen, dazed, searched to piece together Soren's bizarre behavior, which hit her with the sudden sense that much was wrong, though the edges were scattered.

"I said I was your brother, don't worry, but *yes*. I wanted to make sure you were okay, taking the right precautions."

"Precautions?"

Soren tugged at his soft curls. "You said Edouard just lets the house fall into disrepair, so I couldn't stop thinking of you, alone, unsafe at Blanchard House." He stopped his pacing and jolted himself back to the moment. He pulled Maureen into his arm, kissing her. "You silly girl. Don't you know how dangerous it is?"

Maureen kissed him back and then pulled away. "Soren, God Bless America! Can you tell me what you're on about already?"

"Francine!"

"Who the hell is Francine?"

“Oh, Maureen.” Soren hugged her. “You don’t watch the news at all?”

“That’s Edouard’s job.”

Soren squeezed her tighter, pressing his hands into her mane of thick hair. “The hurricane, Maureen. It turned.”

Maureen spun out of his arms. “There’s a hurricane? Coming here?”

“It wasn’t supposed to turn. They said it was headed out the Gulf, toward Texas, and maybe Mexico. I don’t know.” Soren went back to pacing. “They said it’s too late for evacuations. That they didn’t detect the change quick enough. If we go now, we’ll be stuck on the roads when it passes through. That’s what they said. This is all such a mess.”

“But how?” Maureen clutched her purse tight to her chest. She was still wearing her thin jacket as well. Her mind was in multiple places, and she didn’t know where to settle her thoughts.

“I’m sure the governor will make a lovely statement about it later, explaining away any responsibility in this horrific display of incompetence,” Soren replied with an eye roll. “But they don’t know how it was missed. They just… missed it.”

“They? Who is they?”

“The news… the meteorologists… who knows? Does it matter?”

Maureen looked away, thinking. “No, I suppose not.” Her eyes flashed wide in horror. “Olivia!”

Soren stopped her from racing out the door. “No, it’s too late to drive all the way back to New Orleans. Didn’t you notice the wind on the drive out? The color of the sky?”

She had noticed, sort of. But this was the tail end of the storm season, and she’d been more concerned with getting to Soren as quickly as possible. She had things she wanted to say to him, and if she didn’t get them out, she might burst.

“There has to be time,” she insisted, ripping herself away, reaching for the door. “She can’t be there, alone, without me!”

Soren gently put one hand on the door. "Maureen. Do you trust me?"

"Yes, but—"

Soren kissed her. "There's not time. Call home. Let Edouard know you're stuck somewhere, and that he needs to get Olivia to a safe spot in the house to ride out the storm. I know he's not a very good husband, but he will do right by his daughter. I know he will. He's a native, and an architect. He'll know precisely where to take her. He'll know what to do."

"You're serious. You're really serious. There's a hurricane, coming toward us. Now."

Soren nodded. "Category 4, the last the news reported. We can only pray it weakened when it hit land, but it's here." He slipped her hand into his and gave her a reassuring squeeze. "We'll be safe here. There's a study that sits dead center of the house, at the top of the stairs. No windows. I already grabbed the blankets and the rest of the hurricane kit, so all we can do now is... wait. See what happens."

Outside, the wind screamed as it ripped through the row of oaks lining the long drive.

Maureen burst into tears.

CHARLES CALLED, JUST AS CONNOR ARRIVED WITH Irish Colleen. Just as Elizabeth declared everything was in the attic now, and it was time for them to go.

"My son," Charles managed. His voice was hardly recognizable. It had an edge to it, an edge with cracks.

"I have him, Huck. He's safe here. We're going to the attic," Augustus said. A harsh, powerful whistle moved against the house, passing hard through the flora. Elizabeth mouthed from the stairs, *we don't have time for this.*

"I need to talk to him."

"We don't have time—"

"Go get him, Augustus!"

Glass shattered in the kitchen. If he didn't get to Ana now, he'd lose it, and there'd be no returning from wherever he went this time. "I have to go. When the roads clear, I'll bring him back to you. I promise."

A deep sob wailed from the other end. "This is God punishing me, as he did the day I married that hellbeast. Now he's taken my son, and I was *wrong*, and I'll never get to tell—"

Elizabeth ripped the phone away and said, "Save it for when we're not all in mortal danger. Nic is safe. Now go be safe, too, you ape," and slammed down the phone. "*Now*, Aggie!"

"Where's Ana?"

"In the attic, with Connor and Mama. And Bea. She's fine." She raced for the stairs and he followed behind, just as another window turned to shards. Elizabeth screamed, and Augustus pushed from behind, half carrying her as they darted for the attic, and the closest thing they had to safety.

LISETTE SCREAMED FROM THE ATTIC STAIRS ON THE third floor. "Listen to trees! Don't be a fool!"

Cordelia scattered up the staircase, nearly shoving her to the side as she flung herself into the attic. "The only fool here is the man we both fucked hoping it would change our futures for the better."

"Nicolas is in New Orleans!" Charles screamed from the staircase leading down to the second floor. His disheveled appearance, half-clothed, hair affright, knocked the rest of Cordelia's cold words back.

"Which is your fault," Cordelia hissed. "But he's safe, which is more than I can say for you, standing out there like a damned idiot."

"It wasn't supposed to turn."

"Hurricanes, like people, are unpredictable apparently. *Why* are you still standing there?"

Charles' mouth gaped. "And Mama. Oh, fuck it all, my mother is probably alone out there, afraid—"

"No," Lisette called, voice drowning against the insistent whipping of the wind. "I talk to her. She go to Augustus."

"He would've told me that! I just talked to him!"

"You no talk, Charles, you just yell, like a maniac!"

"I'm on *her* side," Cordelia said and started to disappear, beyond his view. Moments later, she peeked her head down. "Charles, you get your ass up here *now*. Do you want your son to have a father or not?"

Charles, dazed, eyes traveling the hall and beyond in haphazard stares and gapes, looked at her.

Lisette screamed as something from the exterior of the house was ripped away, a victim of the storm that was now right on top of them.

"Charles." Cordelia's voice was calm. Even. "Come. Please. Now."

"What if I never see him again?"

"You're a New Orleanian. This is par for the course."

"Everyone else here, you crazy man," Lisette called. "Everyone except... where Richard is?"

Cordelia inhaled a painful sigh and forced a smile as she lowered a hand. "Come on. Come with me, darling."

Richard barreled up the stairs and used his body to propel Charles forward, toward the others, toward safety.

"You're going up there, Master Charles, whether you like it or not!"

"Maureen, where are you?"

Edouard had never answered the phone, in all the time she'd been his wife. He'd never spoken with such urgency. Never expressed even an iota of concern for her well-being. Never acted remotely like he'd acted in his short, demanding sentence.

"Where's Olivia, Edouard?"

"With the staff, in the attic, where I should be. Where you should be! Where are you calling from? Are you with your mother? One of your brothers?"

"I, uh..." Soren beckoned for her to hurry. She could lie, but he knew about this, because he'd given this gift to her. Perhaps the only gift he'd given her. "I'm outside the city. Outside New Orleans. I'm with someone." She glanced at Soren. "I called to tell you I'm safe, so Olivia wouldn't worry."

He hissed something that sounded like *thank God*. "Give me the address."

"Maureen, come on." Soren flashed her an urgent look. "He knows you're safe. Now let's go *be* safe."

"I don't know the address."

"Then tell me who you're with so I can find it myself," he commanded.

Maureen hesitated only briefly before answering, and she told the truth.

Edouard's light pause was hard to read. "I see. Okay. I'll be there soon."

"Edouard, no! It's too dangerous!" Maureen screamed, but the line was dead.

Soren tugged her, and she dropped the phone, torn between one life and another, as a large metal object slammed into the side of the house.

Then it started to rain inside.

Inside the house. Inside, where she was, and Soren was, but Olivia was not, and Edouard, Edouard was coming, he was coming *there*, that was, if he wasn't killed trying.

"Look," Maureen said as she slipped away from reality. "Look how beautiful it is."

The last thing she saw before she completely left her consciousness behind were Soren's terrified eyes looking down into hers.

. . .

THE WORLD WENT DARK. IN THE ABSENCE OF LIGHT, ALL sounds amplified, and Augustus' senses picked up vibrations of terror in a thousand tiny echoes. Every few seconds, even this was drowned out, by the relentless horror beyond their veil of safety.

Ana slept soundly in his lap, blissfully unaware of how close the danger was. How ineffective her father would be at protecting her, should things get much worse.

An orange ball appeared in the harsh darkness as Irish Colleen lit one candle, and then another.

Augustus met his mother's eyes across the cool, damp room. He searched for strength and found only fear.

"Let us pray," Irish Colleen whispered.

CHAPTER 15

Breakdown

Wind lashed the world outside. It whipped through the trees, the carefully tended bird of paradise and lantana. Their blindness to the nature of the sounds, of things unknown smashing into the house, smashing the cars parked along the street, escalated their fears, turning them into an entity all of their own.

For all the cacophony outside the safety of their attic, the silence within was deafening. Nicolas slept, curled into his grandmother's lap, but woke every few minutes, eyes wide, questions he didn't quite know how to form sitting behind his anxious gaze. Bea tended to some sewing she said she'd been meaning to get to, while Elizabeth and Connor both stared into the darker end of the attic, wordless.

Anasofiya whined in his lap, so Augustus lifted her to his chest, whispering soft promises of love and safety into her tiny ears. She was so little; this storm, so big. The entirety of her short life had been filled with constant reminders of all the many predators threatening her safety, both big and small, but nothing so much as this, the culmination of his greatest fear.

Irish Colleen was supposed to be the one who reminded them that this was normal; that, like the storm of '65, they'd endure minor damage, rebuild, and move on. Her failure to provide that reassurance pushed Augustus to the darkest place he'd been since Ekatherina died. It was a place he dared not bring Ana, but he couldn't leave her behind, either.

Ana suddenly burst into tears. The others in the attic stopped their respective escapes to look, and the attention burned a hole in Augustus. His failure as a father, on full display. His failure as a man.

Irish Colleen started to rise, but he silenced her with a firm look. This was his job. The most important job he had, far more than anything he'd created at an office in the Central Business District.

He should sing to her. But what? He couldn't remember any songs, though he knew many, and he could cry himself, for all the frustration of this exercise that was over before it had begun.

But then he did remember a song. From Maddy's collection; the one she played when she'd had an especially awful day and needed to go somewhere else for a while.

Augustus ignored the eyes on him and started humming the first few musical notes to James Taylor's "Fire and Rain."

Day turned to night. Charles knew this because what little sunlight peeked through the hastily boarded window at the top corner of the musty attic disappeared. He had no concept of time. *Was* it night? Or had the storm eclipsed the sun?

Lisette whispered soft words to her belly. Reassurances, promises. At least, that's what he assumed. Charles only heard every third or fourth word, because they weren't meant for him.

He had half a mind to remind her there wouldn't *be* a baby growing in her womb if not for him, but anytime he worked himself up about it, the horrors outside silenced him.

"Lisette, dear, you realize you're not actually talking to a child, don't you?" Cordelia's words came from the dark corner.

He could hardly see her, but he felt her presence; this whole time he'd been aware of it.

Lisette said nothing. Perhaps because Cordelia was still her employer. Perhaps because it wasn't worth it.

But Charles had neither such thing holding him back.

"You could learn a thing or two from Lisette."

Cordelia's laugh emerged from the darkness. "There's an especial irony in these words coming from the man who banished his only son to New Orleans right before a deadly hurricane."

"I've made mistakes," Charles said. "Marrying you, of course, being the most egregious."

"You could've divorced me many times, Charles. It isn't as if I haven't given you reasons. I've given you plenty."

"Is there an insult in there, somewhere?"

"Is there?"

Charles scoffed.

"You know the reason," Cordelia pressed. "You should say it. Make it real. Why not? We have time."

Lisette rocked and continued her whispers, this time in French.

"Anyone hungry?" Condoleezza asked. The soft scratch of wicker followed, as she opened the picnic basket. "Might be a while before we can go downstairs again."

"There might not even *be* a downstairs, woman," Cordelia barked.

"Don't talk to her that way," Charles warned. "Ever. I forbid it."

"You like to put limitations on me, and then never enforce them. After all, I'm here, at Ophélie, aren't I?"

Though it was in the seventies outside before they banished themselves to the attic, Charles shivered. A chill had fallen over the attic, over the past hour. "Some arguments aren't worth the time or energy. What do I care if you're here? Have at it! The house is big. Everyone hates you. Sounds more like a punishment to me."

He could feel Cordelia's icy smile, as she asked, "Lisette, do you hate me?"

"Leave her out of this."

"Lisette, answer the question."

"I no hate anyone," Lisette replied. "I'm afraid. For my baby. For us. That's all I know."

"Maybe not a complete idiot," Cordelia remarked.

"I'll throw you out in the middle of this fucking storm, you evil bitch. Don't think I won't."

"It isn't worth it, Master Charles," Richard ventured. "Let it go. Let go of the past. It won't serve you here, or ever."

"Says the man with the most reason to hold onto the past," Cordelia said. "Richard, who is *probably* your father's brother. Richard and his sister both. And yet, here they are, Charles. Serving *you*. Serving the spoiled remnants of a family who saw their mother fit for use, but not fit for a name. Seems apt, somehow, that you were named for your grandfather, Charles, when you are so much like him."

Neither Richard nor Condoleezza said a word. They never had. They never would.

Charles' shame deepened. The whole family knew this shameful secret. The whole family did nothing.

The family of which *he* was the heir, and the one with the power to acknowledge this and make it right.

So why didn't he?

"Lisette's bastard," Cordelia went on. "Will you give that child the same treatment? No, you'll do better, but that better will be somehow worse. You'll give this child more, but take everything from the mother to do it. See, Charles, you and I both know why you keep me around."

"Lisette agreed to the arrangement," Charles replied, voice cracking. He tried to meet Lisette's eyes, but she hadn't taken them off her belly. "I didn't force her to do anything."

"I don't hear her defending your novel idea."

"She knows better than to rise to your bait."

"Or she knows that your arrangement, no matter how terrible, is all she's got."

Charles' head throbbed. Pressure pushed at his skull. "Shut up."

"She'll be no better than a ghost in this house. No better than one of Sweet Maureen's parlor tricks, hovering, waiting for a moment of usefulness."

"Shut *up*, Cordelia, or I swear to Christ—"

"You'll use her like a brood mare until you've used her up, and then what? Then what, Charles? We both know nothing ever keeps your interest *that* long. Even silly Catherine, the only woman you might have actually, truly, *really* loved. Who broke that off again? It wasn't her. It was your fickle nature. Your inability to give more than you take. You will take everything from Lisette, and then you will leave her with nothing."

Charles jumped to his feet. "I'll fucking murder you with my bare hands if you don't stop running your goddamned mouth, you crazy bitch!"

"Charles," Richard warned but made no move.

"Ahh." Cordelia laughed in the darkness. "And there we are. The *real* Charles. The one who can and has murdered others. You think I didn't know? You think others don't?"

"You're fucking insane, you know that?"

"Augustus only worried about the police. But what of the rest of New Orleans? What of all the others, who know you killed that teacher, Evers, for fucking Maureen? Or those transients, after they attacked Evangeline? To your credit, you did *not* kill the children bullying Elizabeth, but does Colleen know her old lover, that professor, disappeared not long after she left for Scotland? No? Oh. You haven't told her."

Lisette stopped whispering.

Cordelia made a soft sound. "Of course, who could blame you? Anyone who hurts one of your sisters is off-limits. Who could blame you? But what about the one who hurt your brother?"

"You and your incessant fucking *rambling*."

"What about Ekatherina, Charles?"

A thousand tiny pinpricks danced over the surface of his skin. All the air went still, and then was sucked away from him, out of the room, into the storm.

"Charles?" Lisette asked.

"Charles?" Cordelia repeated.

COLLEEN FIRST TRIED TO CALL HER MOTHER'S HOME. A pre-recorded message from the operator told her the phones were down. Then, she stepped aside to let Noah make the call to his father, but when the color disappeared from his cheeks, she knew he, too, got the message.

Magnolia Grace.

The Gardens.

Ophélie.

Even Sullivan & Associates.

All down.

"Jesus," Colleen whispered, falling into the chair. She buried her face in her hands. "What do we do?"

Noah rested both hands on her shoulders and sighed. "We just... we remember hurricanes are a way of life, and they know what they're doing."

"Why isn't the news talking about this?"

"Maybe they don't know about it over here yet." Noah squeezed her shoulders. There was a light tremor in his touch. "Eugenia said the storm turned, and—"

"Eugenia didn't get to finish, because the phone lines died."

"They know what to do. This isn't their first hurricane."

Colleen gazed at him, eyes red. "We also don't want it to be their last."

"What do we do?" It was Noah's turn to ask the question.

"Nothing," Colleen said. "We do nothing, because there is nothing. Nothing we can do. Not from here."

Noah dropped to his knees, bowed his head, and began to pray.

Augustus was on his forty-second iteration of the song. He was surprised he knew the words at all, and wondered if he was even getting them right. More than likely, he'd filled in the blanks with made-up words and made something new, which was okay, too, because a song was a song, and maybe it was better if Ana had something that was hers, and not the hand-me-down of a dead aunt.

"Augustus."

He didn't look up. Connor had been trying to get his attention for a while, but if he stopped singing, Ana would cry, and if Ana cried, Augustus would cry.

"Let me take her for a bit."

"It's quite all right," Augustus replied, rocking his sweet daughter. It was then he realized her head was damp. Covered in it. "Is the roof leaking? Where's the moisture coming in from?"

"The roof is fine, darling," Irish Colleen replied, and he heard in her voice how she held herself back from saying what she really wanted to say, and he both loved and hated her for it.

"You're crying," Elizabeth said. "You got it on her."

"Lizzy," Connor cautioned.

They could both go to hell, as far as Augustus was concerned. Elizabeth, for her flip comment, Connor for trying to protect him. Neither of them knew what he faced every day as the father of Anasofiya Aleksandrovna Vasilyeva Deschanel. They pandered to him, coddled him, and sometimes even scolded him, but that was not the same as knowing. As living it.

But he supposed he *was* crying, and he had gotten it on her. When he went to wipe at his face, there were so many tears that they must've started ages ago, and he wondered if everyone in the attic had a front row seat to his mental collapse, or just his snarky sister.

Connor pressed his hand to the dusty ground and pushed himself up. Without asking, he slid his arms, gently, under the cradle Augustus had made for Ana, and, without asking, he took her into his arms.

"Rest for a bit. I'll give her back. Promise."

Connor carried her to the corner, where he pulled the cover off an old rocker and eased himself into it, holding Ana tight to his chest, supporting her head. All the things Augustus taught him.

Augustus didn't register his mother standing, or coming over, but when she slipped her hand through his arm, he understood that things in the room had shifted. He was no longer the parent, but the child. It wasn't a suggestion of permission, but an order.

Augustus looked away, into the darkness, still crying, but this time he knew about it and could do something. He closed his eyes and, for the first time since he was a boy, searched for God.

As Elizabeth watched Connor tend to Anasofiya, she was rocked with another powerful vision.

Connor, asleep, holding their daughter.

Connor, exhausted, holding their son.

Elizabeth swallowed a painful breath. It trapped in her chest.

Danielle.

Tristan.

Her children.

Elizabeth would die young, but first, she would *live*.

Soren went down to check on the damage when the banging on the door started.

They exchanged looks. Maureen fled down the stairs and unbolted the door.

Before anyone could say a word, Edouard pressed Maureen to

his chest with a firm hand. He ran the other through her hair, just once, and then dropped both his hands to his sides.

"Edouard!" It came out as a whisper. "What happened? How did you get here?"

"I got stuck on the bridge," he said. "I came as soon as it cleared. It's not important."

"But... the bridge!" Maureen envisioned him huddled in his car as the wind whipped the metal over the Mississippi. "You could've died!"

"I didn't die," he replied. He looked past her and nodded at Soren. "Thank you, Mr. LaViolette. I'm taking Maureen home now."

Soren returned the nod, giving Maureen a confused, helpless look, likely wondering if he should argue, if he should come to her, if he should attempt a proper goodbye.

"I'll call you," Maureen said, letting Edouard take her by the hand and lead her away.

Soren, mouth open, bounced his head in acknowledgment.

"I don't think that will be necessary anymore," Edouard said.

CHARLES WAITED UNTIL THE CONVERSATION DIED before slipping away. This time, no one stopped him. Cordelia didn't beckon him to return in that strange softness she'd offered when they went up into the attic, and Lisette didn't beg him to be sensible. Neither of his women seemed to possess much care for his well-being anymore.

But he was still the master of this house, and this family, and if anyone should be the first to emerge into whatever was left of the world outside, it was him.

What about your brother?

What about Ekatherina?

Charles set his jaw and climbed down. Cordelia could go straight to hell. He'd talk to Colin soon about making sure she got *nothing* if he died. There'd be ironclad provisions preventing her from even stepping foot inside this house, or any Deschanel property. Hell, maybe he'd do away altogether with the idea of a singular heir and spread things equally, between his son and daughter, or any other children he might have, should Lisette choose to come near him again.

What about Ekatherina?

Charles hopped onto the carpet of the third floor hall. He glanced around, cautious, as if the storm could be lurking around any corner of the Big House. When things seemed safe, he moved on, down the hall, down the first set of stairs. The second floor looked no more worse for wear, other than a shattered dormer window at the end of the hall.

What about your brother?

Charles descended the final staircase more slowly. In the hurricane of '65, this was where the house took the brunt of the damage, in the front, near the double parlor. His foot crunched through a pile of detritus, debris from the oaks that had blown through a window that had the storm shutters pulled off.

He stopped breathing. Listened.

The wind had died down considerably. It was still there, whipping through the tops of oaks, but it no longer screamed at them, demanding recompense.

With a deep breath, he pulled open the double doors to inspect the damage.

What about Ekatherina?

"What about her? She was killing him. I did what was needed, same as I always have."

Charles stepped outside and released the breath. Well. There would certainly be some cleanup. Bits and pieces of plants, trees, farm implements, all came together in a strange marriage of chaos, littering the property and road beyond, as far as the eye could see. Even the levee was covered in the remnants of those things at Ophélie incapable of holding on.

Richard appeared behind him. Richard, the best man he knew. Richard, his uncle.

"Go on in and comfort that girl, Charles. She's beside herself, and you know how it can be for women, so early in their pregnancy and all."

"Sure." Charles clapped the man on the back. He'd do something about the injustices done to Richard and his sister. He would. God knows why his father never did, but he'd do the right thing. Not today... today they had other things to focus on, like the hellscape outside. "Thanks."

"I'll start inspecting the property, Charles. Go on."

Yeah, technically he *had* killed Ekatherina, but that would infer she wasn't already dead inside when he placed the pillow over her angry, vengeful face.

All his siblings had benefitted from his protection, even if they were unaware.

WINTER 1976

NEW ORLEANS, LOUISIANA
VACHERIE, LOUISIANA
CAMBRIDGE, MASSACHUSETTS
EDINBURGH, SCOTLAND

CHAPTER 16

брат

The letter came just before Thanksgiving.

Elizabeth and Connor—when he wasn't nose-in-a-book studying, or attending classes at Tulane—ran around with an unsettling sense of urgency, getting Magnolia Grace ready for the holiday. Mama had been unwell for a couple weeks, and Augustus knew it was bad when she said she wouldn't be able to host the feast this year. He told Elizabeth to monitor it closely. They could have Evangeline or Colleen home within a day to lay hands on her, if need be. But while she eventually lost the chill and cough, she didn't insist on taking back the holiday, either.

It was times like this Augustus realized that while his mother wasn't old, she *was* getting older.

Augustus was home alone when it came. The name at the return address chilled him to the bone. But this letter came not from Russia, but New York. The first thing he noticed, when he turned over the fine paper in his hands, examining the handwriting, the flow of words, was that you wouldn't know this letter was written by a non-native speaker.

He dropped into his chair at the long dining table, sighed, and began.

Dear Augustus,

This letter will come as a surprise to you. I'd like to begin by offering my family's gratitude for the nice letter we received after Ekatherina's passing. I regret to inform you that the money you sent with it was seized at the border, but you knew that would happen. We appreciate that you tried anyway.

I have accepted an assignment as a clerk at the Russian embassy, in New York City, New York. It's an esteemed role. My parents are proud for me to serve my country, and I look forward to the day I can do what my sister could not and bring them here. I believe the world is changing faster than we think.

The conditions of my visa do not allow me to travel beyond the city. My sister was fortunate enough to secure sponsorship from an American, but that is not how it works for a Russian employed by a foreign embassy. When on embassy soil, we are on Russian soil.

That being true, it is my greatest wish to meet you before my tenure is up. A typical assignment is two years, but they have been recalling comrades back after one. I have been here three months. I do not know how long I have.

Anasofiya Aleksandrovna is my blood, and, on behalf of my family, it would be a great gift if you could bring her to meet her дядя. Her mother's брат.

Yet if you do not come, I will also understand.

твой брат,
Aleksei Aleksandrovich

Augustus set the letter on the table. Next to him, Anasofiya banged her hands into the banana mush she'd made on the tray of her highchair, giggling with inexplicable delight.

. . .

EVANGELINE POURED THE WHISKEY UNEVENLY IN THE two red plastic cups. She never understood the art of a good pour; why it was important. Movies confused her on the subject. Take wine, for example. If you know you're coming back for more, why the pretense of a glass you only fill a third of the way? What was the point of that?

Cassie accepted hers with two fingers on the rim and washed it back, angling the cup toward the bottle for more. Evangeline obliged, this time giving her the amount she should've to begin with.

"To Danica," Cassie said.

Evangeline pressed her plastic cup to her friend's. "To Danica."

She winced after a sip but drank more anyway. "Don't take offense to this question, but why the hell are the police so ineffective against this guy?"

"No offense taken," Cassie said. She leaned back in the chair, elbows propped on the arms, whiskey dangling from one hand. "My father was a good cop, but he was a small-town cop. Petty offenses. Family fights. Dumb shit."

"Sounds nice," Evangeline said, taking another sip.

"It is, in a way. This is nice, too, in a way." Cassie looked down into the cup, frowned, and set it aside. "Everyone fights for their way of life eventually, though."

"What do you mean?"

"That's all small towns are, people fighting to keep things in a bottle, a pocket in time. Preserved, unchanging. And Cambridge? Well, we have pockets, too. We're creating one, now, the two of us, living together. Our way of staying safe, to protect what we love."

"Our lives, you mean."

"More than our lives. We'll survive this, Evie, but we might never be the same. There's no such thing as a single victim in any crime."

"You think so? We'll survive this?"

"You know what I think." Cassie should've been a criminal justice major. She talked a lot about some people at the FBI who were working on a project profiling perpetrators of serious, violent crimes. She was fascinated; had read a book by someone about it, and now seemed as if she might even toss aside all her hard work and apply at Quantico. "He's escalating. He's not in control, like he once was. He used to be so neat and methodical, and now he's leaving messes at crime scenes. Not giving the women the attention he used to, cleaning them up the way he did the first few."

Evangeline rarely had so much to learn from someone else. She'd spent her life being the smartest in a room, at least until MIT, but this was a topic she had almost nothing to contribute to. "How does that help us, though?"

"A careless criminal becomes easier to catch." Cassie passed her cup for a refill. She was drunk, and Evangeline had never seen her drunk. "But he'll kill more before that happens."

Evangeline started to screw the lid back on the bottle, when she realized it was empty. With a scoff, she tossed it toward the trash, missed, then abandoned her interest altogether. "What makes us special?"

"We're ready for him."

Evangeline laughed. "I am *not* ready to meet this Neanderthal!"

"Hey, Neanderthals were more civilized than today's psychopaths." Cassie grinned. "I mean, we're taking precautions. That's all. Other girls are cowering in fear, but we've done a lot, haven't we? You just got your brown belt. We're both sharp shots with our guns. I spent my whole life going over the checklist my father ingrained in me from a young girl. I'm just saying, we're better prepared than most."

Evangeline liked many things about Cassie, but this was perhaps the most endearing. Anything Cassie said, no matter how ridiculous, had an air of confidence that was utterly believable. She didn't know if Cassie gave these reassurances because she meant them, or because she knew it would give Evangeline comfort, but if it worked, did it matter?

But it was this same trait in Cassie that made her feel safe, and she supposed that was why she finally told her the whole story.

Serendipity.

Her minions.

Everything, without holding back. The liquid courage took her halfway, and Cassie, eyes wide with empathy but not sympathy, took her the rest of the way.

"Well, Evangeline, I wish I could tell you the universe was built to limit our suffering. That what happened to you once can never happen again." Cassie bowed her head, dropping her elbows to her knees. "My mother was raped."

"Cassie," Evangeline whispered, breathless.

"She was raped, two years after she married my father, by a man who the state failed to keep locked up after he raped three women years before. She was raped and discovered she was pregnant, and that's how I came into the world."

The blood rushed away from Evangeline's face.

"So my father isn't my blood father. He *is* my father. There is no one else in the world who will ever *be* my father, and that's that," Cassie said. "But I don't have a mother, because a year later, when a jury failed to convict him, he returned and killed her. He slashed her throat in broad daylight and ran away. They never found him. Even if they had, would it matter? The law isn't built to protect us, Evangeline. It never has been."

"God. I don't know what to say."

"There's nothing *to* say. I'd guess the reason you haven't told more people about what happened to you isn't because of a lack of trust, or even shame, but because you don't want to look into someone's eyes as they struggle to adequately express how fucking *sorry* they are."

Evangeline considered this, and it felt right. "There is something I think I should say, though. You won't like it."

"You might be surprised."

"If the universe saw fit to give me a baby after my assault, I would've seen fit to destroy it before it became real."

Cassie smiled. "You think I don't understand that? Just because my mother chose differently?"

"I think it feels insulting to you, after what your mother endured. It makes me seem weak, or even selfish."

"Evangeline," Cassie said with a soft sigh. "I told you my truth. You told me yours. All we have are our choices, and we can't measure our successes and failures and, ultimately, our decisions that led to them from shoes we haven't walked in. I would've aborted me." She grinned. "I'm glad she didn't, obviously, but it took more than great courage to keep me. I know my father looks at me every day and wonders if I'm damaged. Oh, he'd never say it. He wishes he wouldn't think it, either. He'd die for me, a thousand times over. But being a monster sometimes runs in the blood."

"You're not a monster," Evangeline replied, voice firm.

"I know that," Cassie said. "But I was born from one. And I know that, should the occasion arise, I wouldn't hesitate to kill one."

Evangeline thought of Charles, who'd killed, more than once, perhaps way more than once. Was he a monster, when he'd killed only monsters? What would she or Cassie be, if they also took a life, to save others?

"I hope it doesn't come to that," Evangeline said finally.

"Do we have another bottle?"

Charles only half-participated in what Colin called their "old friends reunion dinner." It wasn't much of a reunion, or a dinner, but rather a haphazard attempt at conversation as everyone pretended to be okay while picking at food.

The wine flowed, though, and lots of it.

Colin and Catherine laughed with their mouths, but not with their eyes. If they'd been in the polite company of anyone other than the Sullivans, Charles was certain Cordelia's own dead expression would have given her "charm" away.

It was a farce. An illusion. A bold attempt to restore something that was broken to begin with. They all knew it, but no one said it. No one dared.

"And our counselor, you know, she's a wise woman." Colin smiled at his wife from his peripheral. "Really sharp. She said Catherine needed something outside the home. That I have the firm, of course, but not all women want to stay at home all day. I never thought of it like that, until she said it in those words." Colin talked about his counselor in the way a man who found Jesus might talk about his newfound faith; a little nervous, and a lot hopeful.

"Fascinating," Cordelia said, face in her wine glass.

"I hadn't thought of it that way either," Catherine said meekly. Meekly. Charles had never seen this side of his Catherine. She was the light, not the shadow. She bathed others in her radiance. She didn't hide behind it. "But, of course, she was right. I used to want to be a writer, as we all know." Her laugh broke his heart, but when Colin didn't laugh with her, it gave him hope. Maybe he'd taken Charles' advice to heart, after all, and stopped looking at his wife as a second-class citizen. "That's silly, when I think of it now."

"Not silly," Colin said conciliatory. Trying. He put a hand over hers.

"Silly," she insisted. "But I went to college for a reason. I wasn't a bad student. I liked school."

"I remember," Charles said.

Cordelia made a sound, subtle, but not subtle enough.

"Yes, well." Catherine looked down at her plate and the food she'd hardly touched. "I decided to take some typing classes, and maybe go to business school, if things go well there."

"Night classes," Colin said, unable to resist the urge to clarify her words. *Some things are just too ingrained*, Charles thought. "When I'm at work, she looks after Oz, and then I can come home and give her some relief in the evening. It's perfect, really."

"Speaking of perfect, have you seen pictures of Rory and Carolina's new daughter?" Cordelia said, turning on her best impression of the "human" setting.

Charles wondered when her face would slide off into her meal, revealing her true form.

Catherine visibly paled. She stabbed her fork into some peas.

"What a blessing," Colin said with a sigh, smiling. "Poor Carolina has had such a rough time of it, and we all thought Clancy would be their last. God works in mysterious ways."

"Indeed he does. And might be the first Sullivan baby not to be born looking like he stepped out of a potato field!"

Everyone stared at Cordelia, mortified for similar, but different reasons.

"What? Black hair. Green eyes. Am I wrong?"

"Clancy is blond," Colin pointed out, clearing his throat.

"With green eyes."

"Yes, I suppose his eyes are green," Colin conceded.

"Robyn has the most beautiful golden hair," Cordelia went on, musing, as if she ever mused, ever took time to dream, or consider. "Reminds me a little of yours, Catherine."

Catherine looked as if she might regurgitate what little she'd eaten.

Colin tilted his head and grinned as he regarded his wife. "It is a little like Cat's. But Carolina has the same hair."

"Yes. Of course," Cordelia replied, but shot Charles a meaningful look across the bow.

Catherine stood and excused herself to clear the table. Cordelia dutifully followed, and for a moment Charles almost did as well, for fear of what Cordelia might say to Catherine. He didn't know where she was going with her pointed comments over dinner, but she was gunning for Cat, that was for certain.

As soon as they were safely in the kitchen, Colin's façade crumbled.

"Oh, Huck." He sighed and sank into his hair. "That was okay, wasn't it? It seemed okay. It felt right."

"Dinner?"

"Dinner. Us, all together again."

"If you mean us minus Cordelia, yeah, it wasn't shabby."

"She's certainly an unusual woman," Colin said. Only once had he ever ventured an unkind word about Cordelia, and it was right after he'd learned about her choreographed hysterectomy.

"Weird to see her get excited about a baby she's never met in person when she can't even be bothered to get excited about her son," Charles replied.

"That was strange," Colin agreed.

"Has she..."

"Cat?"

Colin sighed again. He understood the rest of the question, and the questions that would follow. "You know she was at Rory and Carolina's, but if you're hoping for answers, I never got any either."

"She was gone for half a year. More."

"I know."

"Don't you want to know? I'd want to. I'd fucking *need* to."

Colin flashed him a sad look. "You'd be surprised what you think you need, Charles, when what you really need is returned to you. You'd be surprised how much you can overlook, to have something back."

"But, she hasn't said anything? At all?"

"She said..." Colin ran his fingers over his wine glass. "She said she had some growing up to do. And that she expected more of our marriage than she thought I could give."

Charles winced. "Ouch." He drained his wine glass and refilled both their cups.

"Yes, but she was right. *You* were right, when you gave me that advice about how I was treating her. I didn't mean to. I've loved her since... since the first day. Since the first moment. But I wasn't fair to her, and if I want my marriage to work, then this isn't a battle I can win. Even to fight it is to lose."

"That's all she said? Pinned it on you?"

"She didn't pin it on me, Charles. It was both her immaturity and my inability to expect anything less than perfection. She needed time, and I'm not going to push, not going to ask what she did with that time, because she's here now, isn't she?"

"I guess, but—"

"She came back to me, and that's more important to me than answers that will only break my heart."

"You need to make up with Lisette."

Charles pressed the bear to Nicolas' face, wiggling it, searching for a giggle, but Nicolas didn't like that bear anymore. He hadn't for a while, it seemed, because he looked only annoyed and went on to play with the stuffed kitty.

"Come again?"

"You need to make up with your mistress, Charles. And you need to do it before that baby is born."

Charles scoffed. "Things are fine. She's pregnant. Pregnant women are moody."

"Finding out their lover is a cold-blooded killer will do that."

"All bullshit," Charles insisted, but he couldn't look at her. He instead focused on Nicolas, wishing the connection between them was what it once was, and that he had the power to recover what he'd broken in his madness. "Just you grasping at shit that doesn't exist."

Cordelia laughed. "Okay, Charles. But if she goes off script and decides not to play our little game you've set up, where I'm the mommy and she's just the pretty nanny raising our kids, we're going to have a problem."

"She won't."

"Can you be so sure?"

How did Cordelia know so goddamn much? The Evers thing

was a rumor even Augustus couldn't completely kill, but the transient kids? Colleen's boyfriend? *Ekatherina*?

And now, this. He supposed it wasn't exactly a state secret that Lisette had gone cold toward him. The house was big, but not that big. He had the urge to kick Cordelia back to her townhouse in New Orleans, but—and he hated to admit it—she was right. Lisette committing to this arrangement was just as important as Cordelia staying the course.

"Our marriage is what it is, and will never be more than what it is," she said. "But this family is worth protecting. On that, and maybe only that, we can agree."

"Hey, that shit at dinner. What were you on about, going after Cat like that? She's been through enough."

"Of course you'd defend her."

"Cut the shit. You seem to know everything, so you know it's been over between us for a long time."

"Yes, well, some things never *truly* end, now do they?"

CHAPTER 17
The Magi Network

"You can't really be considering this."

"For the last time, Elizabeth, *stop* going through my mail."

"You didn't go to great pains to hide it. In my defense."

"There is no defense. You read my mail. Violated my privacy."

"And damn good thing, too, because now I can stop you from making a horrible mistake!"

Augustus set Anasofiya in her high chair and transferred the soft food to her tray. "I never said what I planned to do."

"Aha!" she cried. "You said *planned to do*, which means, you are in fact, planning to do *something*, instead of nothing."

"You're impossible."

"I'm a voice of reason in a field of bad decisions."

"I see no field."

"You're in it, bro."

"Did you see something? Is that it?"

Elizabeth recoiled. "No, actually, I didn't, or I wouldn't have found it out by reading your mail, would I?"

"Speaking of bad decisions..."

"If you're going to bring up college in order to deflect this conversation back to me, you can stop right there. I don't care. I'm not going. The end. Skip the epilogue and go right to the credits."

"I like how your decisions are beyond reproach, but mine are fair game." Augustus took the small white spoon and turned it into an airplane, winding down toward his daughter's amused mouth. She sputtered the pureed squash back at him, before swallowing some.

"He only wants to blame you. You know that, right? He needs someone to blame, and who better than the infidel husband?"

"If you know him so well, maybe you should've mentioned that. We could've put him on our Christmas card list much sooner."

"Don't be cute. What good can possibly come of someone making you feel worse?"

"We don't know *what* he wants, Elizabeth."

She stabbed at the paper. "He wants to see you. He wants to see Ana. He can't come here, so he wants it on his territory. None of that feels weird?"

"No, actually."

"And when he does hurt you? What then?"

Augustus dropped the spoon. Ana squealed and clapped her hands together, which were covered in orange mush. "I'm a grown man, Lizzy. I can make my own decisions. And where this is concerned, I haven't made one yet."

"But you will."

"I will."

"And soon."

"That a prediction or a question?"

Elizabeth frowned. "More of an allegation."

"Whatever I decide, it will come down to what's in Ana's best interest."

"Good." Elizabeth jumped up, with a crooked smile. "Then we agree."

"Hey," Augustus called after her. "When is the painter coming?"

"Which one?"

"What do you mean, which one? Did we have damage to more than just the shutters?"

"Uh, yeah, Aggie. We did, when the neighbor's thingy smacked into the screened porch."

"Thingy?"

Elizabeth waved her hands. "I don't know what it's called. That farm thingy they were using to redo their backyard."

"Rototiller?"

"I guess?"

"When were you planning to tell me?"

She shook her head. "As with most things, I *did* tell you, and as with most things, you either weren't listening or forgot."

THIS WAS COLLEEN'S FIRST TRIP HOME WITHOUT Amelia. She'd be back, in a month, with Noah and Amelia… and news. News she could share now, but Noah's way of caring for her was standing by her side in all things. It was what love meant to the man whose father had abandoned his love, and later, inadvertently, inspired his son to do the same. Colleen's way of loving him back was to let him do it.

She would've rather waited and come back as a family at Christmas, but these early days as magistrate would set the tone for all that followed. If she showed an inclination to let things slide, and only come back when something happened, everything Ophelia rebuilt for them would eventually dwindle to an afterthought.

The trip was only two days. She spent day one making the rounds to her family, first visiting with Irish Colleen, then Magnolia Grace, and finally, Ophélie. She'd tried to reach Maureen, but the staff said she was under the weather and requested no guests. *Not even her sister?* she'd asked, to which the reply came, *she'll see you at Christmas.*

All the babies in the family weren't babies anymore. Most were walking, all were talking, and they'd started to develop distinct personalities. Nicolas would be the mischief maker of the generation, while Anasofiya possessed a quiet, if inquisitive, strength. Olivia, whom she got to play with at Irish Colleen's, was excellent at manipulation but loved nothing more than to receive more subtle affection, like cuddles. Her Amelia was more like Ana, but already Colleen had noticed that Amelia seemed affected by the emotions of others. She sensed when someone was hiding angst, like a dog could sense a coming storm, as Irish Colleen liked to say.

What type of human would Charles' little one be, coming in a few short months?

And Colleen's new son?

Colleen called the meeting to order, starting with the vows, and jumping right into announcements.

"First, congratulations are in order for Pansy and her husband, Placide," she said with a pleasant smile. "Blessings to you on the arrival of your daughter, Clothilde. I bet Rex is beside himself to have a sister!"

A tired Pansy smiled at her peers. "That little fool's like his daddy. Can't decide what he wants from day to day."

"Gets that from his mama, too," Pierce mumbled, hiding a grin.

"Congratulations to you as well, Papa," Colleen said, turning to him. "Your second grandchild, Pierce. You hardly seem old enough for one."

Pierce flushed. "That's sweet of you, Colleen, but Winnifred reminds me every day that I'm not as young as I think I am."

"Fifty is hardly old, Daddy," Kitty said. "It's not like you've got one foot out the door."

"No, but you'll understand, one day, what it is to begin to

slow down." He patted his daughter's hand, eyes glistening. "But Kitty has good news, too, don't you, sweetness?"

It was Kitty's turn to redden. She paused and then held up her hand with a beaming grin, wiggling her fingers to reveal a glittering diamond.

"Kitty!" Eugenia exclaimed.

"Who's the lucky guy?" Colleen asked.

"Landry Marsolet, that upstart from Gentilly," Pansy muttered, but smiled, too, when Kitty threw her an elbow.

"That's wonderful, cousin," Luther said.

"So? When is it?" Cassius probed.

"We're not in any hurry." Kitty moved her eyes to her father. "Daddy says the family should stay in mourning for two years."

Colleen nodded, thinking to herself that these traditions were no better than superstitions. But sometimes tradition was all they had. When Blanche's third and final husband, Claudius Broussard died, only a month before Ophelia, his loss dealt an awful blow to that side of the family, especially Eugenia, Cassius, and the five children between them. Although Pierce was not Claudius' son, his decision to honor the mourning was out of respect for his mother, Blanche.

"Aunt Blanche will appreciate the honor you give her," Colleen said. "And congratulations, Kitty. It's always a blessing to see this family grow."

"And you, Colleen?" Eugenia nodded toward her belly. "Do you not have an announcement as well?"

MAUREEN FELL INTO A DEPRESSION FOLLOWING THE dramatic rescue at Soren's.

It wasn't like that initially. She was buoyed by the knowledge Edouard *did* care. He did love her, in his own, twisted, unorthodox way. At the thought of losing her, he'd risked his own life, and those were not the actions of a man indifferent.

This was all she'd ever wanted, all along. She'd sacrificed, putting aside her own hatred and resentment at what he'd done to her, and it wasn't so much to ask that he could meet her halfway.

But then, days went by, and nothing changed. They still ate together in their respective silences, returning to their own rooms, living their own lives, separate. The only thing he said to her was that he'd rescinded his permission about Soren, and that he'd like Maureen to stop seeing him. *I can't force you to abide by this, but I'm asking you to put that behind you now.*

Maureen waited for the quid pro quo; what was in it for her, to give up something that made her happy and whole? But it never came, and it was as if that day in Bayou St. John never happened at all.

She didn't ask why. Edouard had never liked to be questioned, and she'd receive no satisfying answer. Every answer to every question for him was some version of *because I said so*, and she could hardly breathe, she missed Soren so much. To hear her husband declare he'd taken that from her, simply because he felt like it, would break her spirit.

He rescued you. You can't forget that.

Maureen hadn't forgotten, though she wished, now, that it had never happened. What good was her husband's moment of exposed weakness if he never showed it again? If nothing changed? If she went back to being the sad mistress of Blanchard House, wasting away her best years while he did as he pleased?

She snuck phone calls to Soren. She wished, now, that she'd told him she loved him. That she'd not been so stubborn about it, waiting for him to say it first. But the phone wasn't the place to say words like that for the first time, and, secretly, she hoped the feelings would just go away. Edouard didn't want her seeing Soren, and without his permission, it was hopeless. She couldn't sneak around town, hiding in dive bars. The practical side of Maureen understood exactly where this would go, how it would end.

But the dreamer in Maureen pictured a life where she and

Soren could run off and raise Olivia, blissfully uncaring about the world they left behind and what others might think.

"Maureen."

Edouard's gruff voice broke through her reverie. She looked down at an entire plate of food, growing cool. How long had they been sitting there?

"Yes, husband." Her voice cracked. If often did now, with her living on the verge of every acute emotion burning within her.

"There's something I'd like to talk to you about." He set his newspaper aside, folded neatly. This was a first. "Something I'd ask you to keep an open mind about."

Maureen's skin was on fire. Her heart leapt around wildly in her chest. He'd never done anything like this, *talking* to her, not without her tentative ask.

"Okay," she said. "I'm listening."

"In your folders, you'll find a list of all our key contacts across the globe." Luther folded his hands and waited while everyone opened the package he'd had printed and set before them. "They've all been notified of the passing of Ophelia, and Colleen's assumption of leadership in her absence."

Colleen watched Luther, a boy on the verge of being a man, but not soon enough, not in his own mind, where he took himself and his work seriously. Where he was the only one in the room in a tailored suit, bearing a posture so erect you'd think he had military training. She should tell him, later, to relax, to take it easy, but all her life Colleen had been told these things and the only message she took from it was that none of the people saying the words understood her at all.

"But," Luther went on, "I believe we have an opportunity to organize these contacts better. I pulled them from the files in the vault, which are, essentially, a more rudimentary form of a Rolodex. Now, all our files need updating. This is a project we'll need to prioritize when we can garner more attendance from the broader Collective, but for now, we need to at least get our contacts in order."

"How often do we even use these contacts, Luther?" Cassius asked. He held one piece of paper aloft, flipping through the folder with his other hand. "For emergencies?"

"This is what I wanted to discuss, Uncle." Luther cleared his throat, a ceremonial social cue Colleen had never understood, more theater than function. "We have an entire network of witches that we do utterly nothing with. I checked, and it seems the last time we contacted any of them was when August Deschanel died. And that was..." Luther checked his notes.

"Nineteen sixty-one," Colleen said.

"Yes, thanks, cousin." Luther looked up. "Fifteen years ago. Fifteen years, and you don't think there's any other use they might have served?"

"Where are you going with this?" Pierce asked.

"A network of witches," Luther repeated. "A wealth of connections. Of allies. Of information."

"Like a coven," Pansy said. "You been watching movies, Luth?"

"Not like a coven," Luther retorted. His jaw was set tight. His muscles flexed under the tension. He was losing his audience, but if Colleen didn't let him find it again on his own, he'd never gain the respect he needed as a Council member. "Think more, United Nations. Not only allies in times of emergency, but in times of strength as well. A network that can learn from one another. Benefit from both learnings and mistakes, and be aware of the world we live in, but also the world *we* live in, which is smaller, more exclusive. Who can tell me how many families of witches are in Louisiana?"

"I don't know. Two. Three," Pierce said.

"Four," Luther answered without checking his notes. "That's not a guess. I know this because of information we gained, inadvertently, through these valuable connections. How many in the United States?"

This time, no one answered.

"Europe? Africa? The world?"

Silence.

"I know we all believe in science. We believe in progress, industry. As men and women, we've benefitted from the broader world as they researched, and learned, failed, and succeeded. But as witches, what do we know, beyond our own borders? Our own bloodlines? What have we learned about what we can do, what others can do, what is possible?" Luther turned to Colleen. "Who do you go to when you have questions about your healing ability?"

Colleen took a deep breath. "No one, I suppose."

"No one," Luther repeated. "I can emphasize. I'm a healer and have no mentor to guide me, to tell me what's possible and not. And Lizzy, how many times has she tried to change the future? She had Ophelia, but who did Ophelia have? Who do any of us have, other than ourselves?"

No one said anything, but Colleen felt the mood in the room shift. She heard them listening.

"The Magi Network," Luther said, coming to his point. "A system of witches, warlocks, or anyone with abilities that the rest of the society wouldn't ever understand. We establish regular contact points, summits, appoint leaders. We assemble."

"Now, uh, Luther, I like where you're going with this," Cassius said. "But this seems bigger than what seven people can accomplish. Don't you think? Why are we the first to try this?"

"We aren't the first," Luther said. "I discovered that when I sent the communications on Ophelia. I had at least eight responses that said they'd tried to connect our world, but Ophelia told them to wait... to wait, presumably, for now."

"But why?" Pierce said. "Why wait, if she agreed?"

"She didn't want to do everything for us," Eugenia jumped in. "She could've left us with so much more, but instead, she left us on the verge of everything. She left us to learn to govern without her, and what Luther is presenting to us now is exactly what she intended."

"Eugenia is right. Ophelia's legacy is this, exactly. It's not that she left us something, it's that she left us in the frame of mind to *make* it something." Colleen's unflinching gaze traveled across the other six, and for the first time, she understood something about what they were doing, something real, something more than just showing up and continuing to do what they'd always done. That's what Ophelia had been trying to say, when she shot down Colleen's suggestions in the meetings and told her there'd be a time and place.

This matter of the Curse. Of the problems plaguing our blood. It isn't a matter of if, my child. It's never been a matter of if. It's always been when.

"I like the idea," Kitty said. "You know how boring these meetings are?"

"Boring means there's peace," Pierce reminded her.

"But ain't nobody learn from times of peace, Daddy," Pansy rebutted. "We sit here with our asses exposed, coming to these meetings, acting like we know they're important, but not one of us can say why, because we've all been damned lucky to grow up when we have. But what about our kids? Memories of the dark ages didn't die with Ophelia. Not if we don't let them."

"It's something to do, in any case," Cassius added.

"Thank you, Luther," Colleen said. A new energy coursed through her. Excitement. Hope. Purpose. They were on the verge of something that would shape the future. "Between now and the next meeting, I suggest we all think of how we'll take this from concept to action."

"We also need to get the Collective meetings going again, Colleen. Get people here, interested again," Pierce said. "Let's not wait for a tragedy to make folks care."

"Agreed."

After, Eugenia lingered to speak with her. Colleen had been hoping she might get a few moments alone with Luther, to give him praise and encouragement, but the look her cousin wore told her this was more pressing.

Eugenia kissed both cheeks and motioned for Colleen to sit down. "I know you're flying to Scotland tomorrow. I won't take much of your time."

"No, it's fine." Colleen straightened her skirt. "What is it?"

"I've been thinking about retiring from the Council."

Colleen's mouth dropped. "What? Eugenia, you're a staple here, you're..."

Eugenia smiled and placed a hand over Colleen's. "I know I was one of her favorites, but that era is over, isn't it?"

"If it's something I did, something I've said, or—"

"No, Colleen. It isn't you." Eugenia flicked at the lapels of her smoking jacket. "It actually has very little to do with the Council, at all. Wallace and I... we've suffered a loss. A rather unexpected one." Colleen didn't probe, but she didn't need to. Her cousin's hand on the belly provided the answer. "A loss that I believe may be a result of the losses of last year. My father. Ophelia. Please don't go spreading this around, as I don't need the family chin-waggers going on about it, but I spent a week in the hospital for exhaustion. It's all had an effect on my health that has reminded me that my boys deserve a mother. They deserve to have me around for as long as God decides to give me, and... truly, Colleen, don't look so grim. You know how I hate sympathy. It's just time. Everything has a season." Eugenia rose. She'd discussed some of the worst parts of her life so clearly, succinctly, and without hesitation, and it was this trait Colleen had always admired in her cousin. That she'd miss the most.

"When?" Colleen asked.

"Soon. Not today." Eugenia smiled. "I wouldn't leave the Council without a replacement ready. I'm giving you time to think about that."

"Luther," Colleen blurted after Eugenia. "You should be proud of him after what he did today."

Eugenia turned, one hand on the doorframe. "Oh, I am. I

never doubted he was the right choice, Colleen. Not once. But it wasn't my job to sell it. Ophelia gave these trials to you."

"I'M LISTENING," MAUREEN REPEATED.

"You're wondering why I took something from you."

"Yes," she said. She lifted her chin. "Actually, I am. I thought we had an agreement."

"We did," Edouard said, nodding. "You know I never wanted this marriage."

"Thanks for the reminder," Maureen muttered before she could stop herself.

"I don't say that to hurt you," Edouard went on. "I have never, not once, said something with the intention of hurting you. That's not who I am."

The tears happened so fast she had no time to stop them. Her lip quivered; the courage came from somewhere. Soren, perhaps, though he was miles away. "But you did hurt me. You hurt me... back then. In the office."

Edouard bowed his head. "I misread—"

"No!" Maureen shot to her feet. "You misread nothing! You took it from... from something we both wanted and you *hurt* me! And *then,* and *then,* I couldn't even move on, because there was a child, and then a marriage, and here we are!"

Maureen's chest heaved with emotion. She'd never done this before; never done anything remotely like it, and she was afraid, and emboldened, and knew that, even if there were consequences, they'd be worth it.

Edouard looked up. He met her eyes. Not even when they exchanged vows had he ever done so. "Okay. You're right. I hurt you. I won't make excuses for it."

"Thank you," Maureen whispered, breathless.

"What remains unchanged, however, is that our marriage isn't what either of us had in mind. For me, I simply never wanted a wife. For you, your ideal is far different than what I've been able to give you." He paused, to gauge for her reaction.

"Go on. I'll stop you when you've said something wrong." She wiped at her runny nose.

"I have unusual tastes. You know that."

"And I have needs. You know that."

"Yes. And... I believe there may be a way to make both of us satisfied. Maureen..." Edouard folded his hands and looked away. "I do care for you. Not in the way you want, but you're my wife, and you're the mother of my child, and your well-being is a matter of concern to me."

"I was fine with Soren. I didn't ask you for anything else."

"You didn't. But all men eventually realize what they may lose, and good men try to fix it." Edouard flashed what Maureen thought might be a smile, but since she'd never seen him do it, she couldn't be sure. "I would like to be able to satisfy you myself."

Maureen *harrumphed.* She'd never exhibit such boldness in her marriage again, she was certain of it, but she'd take this as far as she could while the courage was still in the tank.

"I want to propose that you can still have Soren, but in a different way."

Maureen folded her arms. Watched him.

"I'd like to watch."

Maureen's self-righteousness folded in an instant. "You *what*?"

The silence that ensued, when a staff member came in to refill their drinks, was so painful Maureen could scream.

"I want to watch you make love to Soren. I believe that, in doing so, it may trigger tastes in me that are more typical. Ones you're more accustomed to."

"You want..." Maureen's head was a mess of questions, of disconnected thoughts. "You think watching me with Soren will make you want me?"

"I believe it may."

"You're serious."

"Maureen, I've been accused of many things, most true, but having a sense of humor is not one of them."

Edouard pushed his seat back. With both hands, he dabbed the cloth napkin at the corners of his mouth, then folded that into an even neater version of the triangle the placing was set with. He stood, affected a slight nod in her direction, and then left the dining room, just as the clock chimed ready for him to move on to the next phase of his evening routine, office time.

CHAPTER 18
Peace of Mind

"Mrs. Jameson." The doctor turned to Noah. "Mr. Jameson. Congratulations! I'm happy to confirm your suspicion and deliver the happy news."

"When?" Colleen asked. Both her hands stretched above her, intercrossed, laced through Noah's.

"Oh, we'll need to do a thorough ultrasound, of course, but I'd say late March, early April." He closed his notebook and smiled. "A springtime baby. Always a blessing."

When he left to give them some privacy, Noah pulled Colleen in closer, enveloping her. "I know you're scared."

"I'm not scared." She squeezed his hands tighter when she felt a tremor start.

"You are," Noah said. "It's okay to be scared. We can be happy and scared at the same time, right?"

"We barely have time for Amelia."

Noah released her and knelt in front instead. "Colleen. Amelia is thriving here. She's a happy, well-adjusted baby, in good health. We're parenting *and* pursuing our futures."

"We hardly ever see each other," Colleen said. "I take day classes, you take night classes. If not for the nanny, we'd be a mess, but that's a whole other problem isn't it? Amelia probably thinks Saoirse is her mother, for crying out loud."

"That's not true. She likes Saoirse, but who does she get excited for?"

"You."

"Stop."

"Stop what?"

"You know good and well what." Noah rolled her hands over in his. Kissed them. "Our life is good. It's okay, to have life just be good. We don't always need a disaster to fight."

Colleen looked at him. "Is that what you think I do?"

"Sometimes," he said. "I suspect you think it's the only control you have, fixing what's broken. But you're wrong."

"You're so wise, are you?"

"Not so wise," Noah said, this time kissing her on the mouth. Her cheek rested gently in one palm. "But I know you. And I know us, and I know that a blessing is what we make it. We'll love this baby as we love Amelia, the world will keep spinning. You'll keep stressing, and I'll keep pretending I'm not, and we'll keep on building this beautiful life we chose, together."

"A boy," Colleen said, clearing through the lump in her throat. "We're having a boy."

"I won't be so outnumbered, anymore, Deschanel. Better watch it."

"I'll do you one better and let you name him."

"Benjamin," Noah said, without hesitation.

Colleen cocked her head. "You've been waiting for this. What's the significance?"

"There isn't any," Noah said. "Sometimes a name can just be a name."

"But you *have* thought of it."

He nodded. "I have. And I thought, if we have more kids, we should consider not putting the pressure of living up to their ancestors on their shoulders. That we should throw aside any Irish or French names altogether, and go with something solid and utterly unremarkable."

Colleen watched her husband. *Husband*, a word she still struggled to wrap her mind around, that she, Colleen, could be satisfied, could feel love that wasn't simply dutiful, but vulnerable and raw. "You know there's nothing unremarkable about Benjamin. He was the son of Jacob. Went on to form one of the twelve tribes of Israel."

"And now," Noah said, twining their hands together, pulling Colleen closer. "Our *son*."

MAUREEN HARDLY GOT THE "HELLO" OUT OF HER mouth before Soren had her in his arms, lips pressed to hers between whispers of words that sounded an awful lot like *I love you*.

"You're here," he said, taking a breath, holding her at arm's length as if taking her in for the first time. "He let you come."

I love you, Maureen said, in her head, but what came out was, "Yes, but not without an ulterior motive, I'm afraid."

"What kind of ulterior motive?" Soren slipped her purse off her shoulder and hung it on the rack. "Come, I have a pitcher of mint julep in the parlor."

Maureen followed him, all the while, as she had on the drive over, wondering just what she would say, and how she'd say it. If she acted like Edouard's request was crazy, which it was, she risked Soren saying no and never seeing him again. But if she lied, he would know, because there was nothing, not a single thing, about Edouard's proposal that was remotely normal, or okay. It took something important to her and reduced it to something dirty and unclean. It reminded her of who he was, and how she'd gotten here.

Soren poured her a glass and handed it to her as he sat next to her. She'd never liked liquor, and mint made her gag, ever since her pregnancy with Olivia, but this was his first act of caring for her in over a month and she wouldn't take that from him.

Maureen winced through a deep sip. "He says I can still see you."

Soren's face dissolved in relief. "Thank God. I know we said this was just fun for us both, but it's not, is it? Not anymore." He touched her cheek. "Not for me."

Maureen dropped her eyes, focusing on the ice in her glass, hued in green from the mint. "Not for me, either. But it's not so simple. I've told you about him. About..."

Soren nodded.

"I don't know what's gotten into him. He's... changed since the hurricane, but also not changed at all. He's more protective of me, but only in the restrictions he's placed on me, not in the way *he* treats me himself. Not in any meaningful way, that might feel good."

"He realized he loves you," Soren said. "Must have been some revelation for him."

"I don't think he's happy about it," Maureen said. "He'd just as soon go around assaulting his secretaries in ignorant bliss."

Soren squeezed her leg.

"I also don't think anything has changed. Not *really*. He's only afraid, now, of losing me, or losing a mother for Olivia."

"Don't sell his affection for you too short. Is it so crazy to think he might really care for you? Not in the way I do, or the way most men care for the women they love, but everyone speaks differently when they love."

"He raped me, Soren. Don't make excuses for him."

Soren's face fell. "I'm so sorry, Maureen. I was trying to make you feel better, so you know whatever the shortcomings of the man, they're not yours."

"I know that," she said. "I knew it then, too, but until now I never expected he'd turn a corner, and he has, but it comes with a price."

Soren didn't interject this time. He let her speak, and when she was done telling him about Edouard's sordid proposal, he moved to the side of the couch, hands running down the length of his face.

"I shouldn't have come here." Maureen jumped up. "I don't even know why I told you. The whole thing is so absolutely positively—"

Soren shook his head. He joined her on the carpet. "It's only absolutely positively whatever you were about to say if we care what society thinks."

"What are you... what are you saying? That you *want* Edouard to watch us?"

"I don't *want* him to, *ma cher*, but this is progress for your husband, don't you see? He's never going to be the man you wish he'd be, but he might become one you can live with."

"I don't see how him watching us have sex accomplishes any of that."

"You've seen things in this world, Maureen, but so have I. And my experience tells me this is a bigger step for Edouard than it will be for you. And I don't want to scare you with my predictions, but I think this will be the beginning of something beautiful."

Maureen wrinkled her face. "I don't see how."

"Do you trust me?"

"Of course I trust you, but that has nothing to do with this."

Soren leaned in to kiss her. "I only want you, Maureen. But if I have to go through Edouard to do it, then I will. And if at any time, you're uncomfortable, we stop. No matter what. No questions asked. I want you to have peace of mind, Maureen. Okay?"

Maureen had come here looking for Soren's guidance on another way to keep what they had, but instead he'd sold her on the efficacy of Edouard's insane proposal.

Was she really going to do this?

"Peace of mind," Maureen mused. "Like that song on the radio."

"Yeah," Soren said. "Boston."

. . .

Charles paced around the quad at Loyola University. He didn't know this campus the way he knew Tulane, where he'd misspent more years than he liked to admit. But Cat chose it for a reason; a reason he might've known if they were talking. Maybe her parents had Jesuit ties, or maybe she was just sick and tired of Tulane, that old, esteemed college all her husband's family had such a hard-on for.

He didn't know what building she took her business classes in, but he knew how to use a phone to ask, so he waited, as the light winter wind shimmied through the oaks, swaying the Mardi Gras beads that lived among the branches in perpetuity. It wasn't cold, but the light, electric bite in the air sent chills through him.

Charles rubbed his arms. He should've worn a jacket. Young men and women shuffled past him, less chatty and more purposeful at this time of night. The women tucked their faces down and moved without eye contact. The young men kept an eye out for them, though who was to say one of them wasn't a predator themselves? Like that sicko killing women out by Evangeline. Oh, he tried to convince her to come home, but trying to tell Evangeline *anything* was like speaking French to a dog that learned its orders in Spanish. She didn't know he'd hired someone to watch after her, but the guy was a student himself and still had classes to attend.

He pulled out his pack of smokes, started to shake one out, then slipped it back in his pocket. With a grunt, he leaned into the tree and instead of breathing in toxins, he let the thick, night air roll through his lungs.

"Huck?"

A voice that had stopped his heart, over and over, but this time only startled him. He'd expected to see her first, to have the upper hand.

"Hey, Cat."

She looked around. "What are you doing here?"

"What would you say if I told you I'm a changed man? Going back to school to find myself and all that?"

Catherine's laugh echoed through the trees. "I'd say you're up to your usual bullshit."

Charles laughed in return. "You'd be right. Let me drive you home."

She eyed him, wary. "*Why* are you here?"

"To see you."

"Oh, come on. We're going to do this, here? Again?"

"It's over," Charles said. "We both know that. It's been over. But I have questions."

Catherine rolled her eyes. She pressed her textbook to her chest, and he reached over and took it from her, slipping it under his own arm. "You have questions. Who says I have answers?"

"Your husband might overlook his suspicions, but I won't."

"Which is it, already? Are we over? Are we not? Because if I'm not yours, you're not entitled to anything!"

"Neither is Colin, apparently. You disappeared for *six months*, Catherine, and you just expect everyone to accept you were with Rory and Carolina?"

"You don't have to believe me. Ask Rory."

Charles tapped his head. "See, that's the part I haven't quite figured out, why Rory would lie."

"Rory doesn't lie. We both know that. Remember, he's the reason we broke up the first time."

"Don't blame Rory for your weakness."

Catherine reached for her textbook, but he dodged her. "I don't have to take this, Charles."

"No, you don't."

"Great, we agree. Give me my book."

"Where were you Catherine?"

"My *book*."

"Or, perhaps the better question is, who were you with?"

Catherine stopped reaching for her textbook. She choked out

a laugh, shaking her head. "You think I have *another* lover on the side?"

Charles set her book on the bench behind him. A challenge. "You tell me."

"Why do you even care? So what if I did?"

"So you did."

Catherine glared at him in the darkness. "You are unbelievable." She shoved past him and went for her book, her heat transferring to him as they made contact.

Charles followed her as she marched away from him, down the quad, her feathered hair catching the wind. "He deserves better!" he called, several paces behind.

Catherine spun around. "Colin does? Or do you mean that you deserve to know where I'm at, and who I'm with, at all times? That you don't want me, but you still want to control my life?"

"Colin is my best friend."

"Oh yes, you've proven that *so* many times."

"It's for him that I left you!"

"I don't believe you."

"Tell me, Cat, why else would I? What other reason could I have, to turn my back on the only woman I've ever loved?"

Catherine's chest heaved. Her breath spiraled in the air before her. "What about Lisette?"

"What about her?"

"You love her."

Charles threw his hands up. "Shit, I'm sure trying to!"

"What does that mean, exactly?"

Charles sniffed, an old habit, but one he'd never really lose, because he now knew that the sniff was a cry for relief, whether it came or not. "Because I have to love her, Catherine. Men aren't meant to be alone. Everyone loves someone."

Catherine softened, but she made no move to narrow the gap between them. "That's really sad, Huck. But coming here, questioning me, it won't help anyone. You told me we were done. I believed you."

"I meant it," Charles said weakly, and he wished he could redo the moment because he did mean it, but he couldn't make himself sound convincing.

"You're not entitled to know anything about me. Not anymore."

"Yeah, and Colin? What's he entitled to?"

Catherine smiled sadly. "He hasn't asked, because he knows that if you ask a question, you get the answer, whether you're ready or not." She tucked a bang of hair behind her ear that the wind picked up. "Go home to Lisette."

Charles didn't stop her when she walked away this time.

Augustus tried to recall a time when he'd been on a train. The few times he'd traveled as a child had been by car or plane, and then, as an adult, a businessman, he was exclusively a flier.

He'd rather have flown. Aside from being quicker—a couple hours, rather than a day and a half—flights were a known element to Augustus. Statistically, they were far more likely to perish in a car than a flight, and trains were somewhere in the middle of that.

But Anasofiya was prone to ear infections, something Irish Colleen assured him was normal, but this put a damper on flying when the doctor said it could cause permanent damage to her eardrums. He also said it might not, but that there just hadn't been enough studies done yet to take that risk.

So, Augustus bundled up his daughter, packed their bags for a short trip, and left on the 5:00 a.m. bound for New York City.

Lizzy would be angry when she found his note. Not immediately, of course. The note said simply, *call Mama.*

Irish Colleen knew his travel plans. She knew because he sought her counsel on this, despite that his mother claimed he never needed her. That wasn't true at all, though. He did, when he thought she had something to offer, and on this, he suspected she just might. An immigrant herself, who'd never been back to

Ireland to see any of the relatives she left behind, he wanted to know if she resented her mother for that.

"Resent? No, no, I didn't resent her. I don't," Irish Colleen had said, two days prior, steam from her coffee fogging the glasses she now had to wear. "She made the decision she felt was best, and as a mother who's had to do that far too many times herself, I understand."

"But?"

Irish Colleen exhaled. Her eyes closed. "But, I wish I could tell her she didn't need to protect me. I'm Colleen Brady, and I have people, somewhere."

"You could go back now."

His mother's eyes were heavy. "No, darling. I can't. In the beginning, I might've re-forged the bonds we broke when we fled Ireland for a different life. Perhaps. Who can say? But no, not now."

"You think I should take her."

Her hands, gnarled from years of labor and rearing seven children, curled over his. She was so young still, but not young enough. "I think you knew what you wanted to do before you came over here."

"Still. I need your advice, Mama. Please."

Irish Colleen nodded slowly. "My advice is to take her. Not because I believe she'll remember it, or it will even be good for her. She's too young to hang on to this memory. You take her because it's what *you* need, and if you don't go, you'll never know what could've been. This might be your chance to connect Anasofiya to that half of her heritage. Or? Or, I suppose, it could be the best way to close the door on it. When you meet this young man, you'll know which way that pendulum should swing."

Anasofiya napped in the portable cradle Augustus brought for their train cabin. As they passed through Virginia, the rolling snowy hills brought him peace, however temporary.

CHAPTER 19
New York, New York

Aleksei Aleksandrovich was the spitting image of his sister, Ekatherina. He had the same eyes, cautious and mistrustful, but possessed a glimmer of hope. Same bone structure, delicate and sharp, like what the outside world pictures when they think of a Russian ballerina. Unlike her, his hair was red, which left Augustus wondering which side of the family Ana's coloring came from. There were redheads in his mother's direct line as well, but very few amongst the Deschanels.

This was the first question Augustus asked, when they settled into the bar area of the Waldorf-Astoria. Aleksei had offered his apartment, and Augustus saw no reason to think there was danger in going, but choosing the location restored some of his control in the situation. He knew this hotel. Had stayed there, done business in the bar. It was as close to familiar territory as he had in a city he rarely visited.

"Do either of your parents have red hair?"

Aleksei paused for a moment and then smiled. "Ana. You want to know where Ana gets it. Yes, my *mammochka* has red hair, Augustus. Her mother did not, but her grandmother was a redhead. We did these exercises in science class—"

"Punnett squares."

"Yes!" Aleksei lit up, shaking his finger. He was dressed in the neat, but bland uniformity of the Soviet Union, wearing a hammer and sickle pin at his lapel. A good son of Lenin. "Those. And my teacher said it was not common for both me and Anasofiya—our Ana—to have red hair, but it does happen. We must have strong genes for your Anasofiya to have this."

"My mother's mother had red hair," Augustus said. He dangled one hand over Ana's carrier, to let her play with it. She clasped his fingers in his, squeezing. "So maybe she got it from her."

Aleksei nodded, considering this. "Yes. Yes. I see how that would be possible. She looks so much like our Kat. But, yes, I see you as well. I would so very much like to hold her before we depart."

"She's fussy around strangers."

"Oh. I see. Well, what else can I tell you about your daughter's family, brother?"

Augustus pulled his hand back and gave Anasofiya a teething ring in its place. He had toys in every pocket now, including the ones he didn't even know he had. She sucked on it and stared up with her intense blue eyes. "I didn't come all the way to New York to talk about the family. I came because you asked, and because you have something to say."

"Oh." Aleksei's face fell. "I do have things to say, and I'm glad you came." When a waiter passed by, Aleksei politely grabbed his attention. "Stolichnaya. Two cubes of ice. And you, Augustus?"

"What he's having is fine," Augustus said, though the last time he'd had grain alcohol he'd nearly brought up the remains of his lunch in the breakroom sink.

"Do you drink vodka, Augustus?"

"Not really."

Aleksei said to the waiter, "Add whatever Americans enjoy with their vodka, to his." When he was gone, he asked Augustus, "Have you been here? To New York City?"

"A few times, for work."

Aleksei looked around in wonderment, as if the hotel bar was the city come to life. "And? Is it the magic everyone says? Will I find love? Fall in love?"

Augustus shifted in his seat. Beside him, Ana was lost to her teething bliss. "I wouldn't know. When I come here for work, that's what I do."

Aleksei pointed a finger. "That is very Soviet of you."

"I'm not keen on being compared to the regime that kept me from bringing you and your family here, all the while starving them near to death."

Aleksei's smile faded. "There are a lot of ears in New York, Augustus. We are all comrades."

"You can continue to live in whatever illusion you like," Augustus replied. "I did everything I could for Ekatherina's family. Everything in my power and then some."

"They know. I know. Yet that isn't how this world works, and we both know that."

"I know that now. I didn't know when I married her, or I wouldn't have made such promises..."

"She knew. She blamed you because..." Aleksandr. "I get ahead of myself. How was your trip here? Was the train comfortable enough?"

"The trip was fine. But again, this isn't what we're here to discuss, is it?"

Aleksei accepted his drink from the waiter, and Augustus did the same.

"No. It isn't."

Evangeline and Cassie huddled around the fireplace in near darkness. The police orders were clear: bolt the doors, kill the lights. With the curtains drawn, a thin line of moonlight spilled across the floor, offering the only relief from the blindness.

Cambridge winters were not like New Orleans winters. Back

home, they still, on some days, wore shorts and sandals in December. But here, even a few minutes without heat was unbearable. With the fireplace off-limits, due to the light it would bring, they put all their hope in the space heater that worked only after about thirty seconds of physical assault. They took turns trying to mask the sound of banging, their fear and cold fighting for dominance.

Evangeline pulled all the blankets off their beds, and they created a nest, but it didn't stop their breaths from swirling in the dark air, reminding them that, until this was over, they were prisoners.

"Do you think we'll be able to fly home tomorrow?" Cassie whispered.

"I don't know," Evangeline said, voice so low she couldn't hear her own words. "I wish they'd tell us something. Anything at all."

"If he's out there, he's scared."

"Scared? The killer?" Evangeline would laugh if she wasn't so cold.

"It's a good thing," Cassie reassured her. "He's never been scared before. He couldn't do what he does if fear had ever guided him."

"Because he's a psychopath," Evangeline said.

"Yes," Cassie said carefully. "Though not all psychopaths seek to hurt others. Not all of them become killers. Thankfully, only a few of them do."

"You know a lot about this for a chick from small town Oregon."

Cassie smiled. She exhaled. "I've been thinking a lot, Evie. About us, about who we are, what we've been through, how it's shaped us. I feel safer with guns in our house, and knowing how to fight, but I don't feel *better.*"

Evangeline fumbled under the couch for the bottle of whiskey that had rolled there a week or so ago. She'd forgotten it until now. She uncapped it and took a swig, passing it to her friend. "What do you mean?"

"Safety is a physical thing. But what about the psychological effect? Am I fixed?" Cassie took her sip and passed the bottle back. "No, I'm not. My body is safe, and my mind is stuck in a prison I can't break out of."

Evangeline was glad, for the first time that night, for the privacy the darkness afforded. Even with Cassie, whom she trusted implicitly, she didn't want to share the full extent of her helplessness. She wished Cassie hadn't said this, because, now, the thought burrowed inside of Evangeline and took root.

My body is safe, and my mind is stuck in a prison I can't break out of.

Knowing how to shoot felt good. The raw power of steel and gunpowder, ricocheting from her near-perfect aim, was real and tangible. But a gun protected her from the future, not the past. Knowing how to pick, punch, and pin increased her chances of survival from something not-yet-transpired; it didn't erase the trauma that took root and became part of Evangeline, before she could stop it.

"Evie?"

"Yeah, I'm here."

"I struck a nerve, didn't I?"

"It's fine."

"No, it's not fine." Cassie reached through the blanket and squeezed Evangeline's ankle. "It's not fine, and that's the problem."

"I don't like problems that come without solutions, Cassie. Never have. I can't live in a world where there aren't answers."

"It's why we love science," Cassie said. "But maybe there are answers... maybe they're just not the ones we thought."

Searchlights beaming back and forth outside drove them both into momentary, breathless silence. They were just outside the apartment, down on the ground. Evangeline and Cassie passed a shared terror between their gazes. *Is he here?*

But then they were gone again, moved on. No further instruction, no news, just a drive-through that stopped the hearts of everything nearby.

"I'm leaving here," Cassie blurted. "I've been thinking about it for a while."

Evangeline sighed. "I know. I've known for a long time. Quantico, right?"

"I applied, and they want me to come down in the spring for an interview. I have to pass a ton of background checks on me, my father, my cousin I haven't seen since I was running around in diapers." She cracked a smile. "But I want to do good. What's happening here in Cambridge is horrible, and if I can be a part of preventing it... of helping create systems that make it harder for these monsters to do what they do... that's how I'll survive, Evangeline. That's how I'll break free of the prison."

Evangeline pulled her blanket tighter around her neck.

"Come with me," Cassie said, growing excited. She rolled forward. "Come with me, Evie. We can do it together."

Evangeline shook her head. She didn't need to think about this, despite how painful it would be to say goodbye to her only true friend. She didn't belong in law enforcement. She was a scientist. "I want to stop it, too, but there's more than one way. There's still so little we know about the human brain."

Cassie clasped her hands around Evangeline's. "You're right."

"But there's more," Evangeline said. She didn't know she'd been slowly coming to this, for months. She didn't know, even as she saw the smiling faces of women who'd been raped, and then murdered. She didn't know, even when she met one of the survivors, through the work she and Cassie did as volunteers. "The ones who live. They need to know they're not alone."

Cassie nodded, listening.

"I want to find a way to work with them. To help them see that there are many ways to survive something terrible, and that there *is* a way forward."

"I want that, too." Evangeline couldn't see her face, but she could hear Cassie crying.

"I always wondered, you know, what I'd do with all the family money. I have no use for money, not the kind in my trust fund anyway, but I could start a foundation... a safe place for women who've been raped and don't know where to go next, or don't have anyone in their lives who understands their pain."

"We can," Cassie said. She sniffed. "Together. Even if I'm there and you're here. Virginia isn't so far away. Maybe we met for a reason, Evie. Maybe more than just us both needing a friend, we needed a partner for something bigger."

"I don't want to be in this prison anymore," Evangeline said, because she needed to hear her voice say the words aloud to believe them. "I want to break out. I want to help others break out."

"So sayeth us both," Cassie whispered and nuzzled her face into the side of Evangeline's neck, both falling quiet as the police again came on the bullhorns to remind them to stay inside, bolt the doors, and kill the lights.

"YOU CAN'T JUST DISINHERIT YOUR SON."

"I didn't use the word disinherit. You did."

"I used the word," Colin replied, a careful edge to his voice, "because that's effectively what you're describing, Charles."

Charles snorted. "I simply want to get rid of a tradition that's outdated and boring. Why does it have to be the son who inherits everything? And why just one heir?"

Colin leaned forward, spreading his forearms over his desk. "Nicolas isn't the heir because he's a boy. He's heir because he's the oldest." He pointed at a thick file, punching the manila cover with his finger. "And let's not forget, the estate has never forgotten the siblings of an heir. Look at what your own sisters and brother received. Millions, Charles. The heir doesn't get it all. The heir is a designation. A way of assigning lead, and having someone who is always in a position to guide with authority."

"And we've done it that way, why, Colin? Remind me? Because it's what we've always done?"

"Charles, Lisette hasn't even given birth! Why are we talking about this?"

Charles crossed his arms. "I never liked tradition. What's the point?"

"A lot of people see the point in tradition. Tradition guides the world. It has most certainly guided your family."

"And now, I'd like to change that tradition."

"No."

Charles laughed, rolling forward. "I'm sorry, did you say no?"

"I said no."

"Then I'll go to your father."

"And he'll say no."

"He *can't* say no, Colin! This tradition you have such a hard-on for, it makes it so he can't say no to me!"

"He can," Colin said, fighting to stay calm. "And he will. There are provisions in the estate—"

"Oh, *fuck* provisions!"

"Provisions," Colin went on, "that give Sullivan & Associates some degree of power of attorney if we feel the heir is acting in a manner that is not in the best interest of the estate. Power of attorney that can be further secured with cooperation from the second-in-line."

"Augustus?" Charles laughed. "He would *never* turn on me."

"Like me, he's confused about your hot and cold relationship with a little boy who's done nothing wrong."

Charles threw out his arms. "And why should Nicolas get everything, just because he was first?"

Colin, without missing a beat, replied, "Then why should you?"

Charles sputtered through a series of half-formed words. Self-righteous Colin, once again, standing between him and a decision. Colin, whose marriage Charles had *saved*, and he'd never know it.

Colin, who could wipe that smug look off his Irish face before Charles did it for him.

"I don't know what's gotten into you, Huck, but for a while, I saw the man who was born to lead his family. Now, he's gone away, gone on vacation, gone *somewhere*, and you need to get him back. For yourself. For the family. For Nicolas, and yes, even for your unborn child." Colin leaned back and folded his hands, resuming his initial calm control. "You're acting like a tyrant who's gone off his rocker. Like... like Henry VIII, when he broke from the church and gutted the monasteries. Is that really what you want? To tear apart your family, because you look at that sweet, loving boy and you see Cordelia? Have you forgotten who you are? Who he is? Who your family is? Nothing is stronger than that. Don't punish him and ruin what good you have in you, to punish *her*."

The tremors started in his thighs and traveled out and up. Charles ground his fist into his quadriceps, squaring his jaw, searching for the control he brought into this goddamn office. All the while, Colin watched him. Colin, always fucking Colin. Colin, with the honor and the answers; with the moral compass that left no room for argument.

Charles pushed himself forward and left the room without another word.

MAUREEN CURLED UP IN HER BED, TEARS STAINING HER pillow. It would dry, just as her tears did, but that didn't mean she was healed.

You have the power here. The power to go. To stop. To slow down. To speed up.

It was a lie, all of it. Soren meant the words, but they weren't his to say. Not his promises to make. Agreeing to Edouard's arrangement meant playing by his rules, and his rules had never been fair. They weren't written to accommodate the other players, only himself and his whims, his cruelty buried in sexual expression.

And now, the experience burned within her in a way even that day in his office hadn't. Edouard, standing in his pressed suit, arms folded. Edouard, always in command, even when you forgot it. Soren's confidence faded and he became compliant, forgetting what he'd promised Maureen, or perhaps simply unable to deliver now that the moment was upon them and the power balance established.

Bend her over my desk. Panties off.

No, thought Maureen, though she slid her panties to the floor dutifully. As she, with nary a second's hesitation, settled herself over the desk in his office, soft, cloying papers stuck to her face. Soren's soft hands traveled across the arcs of her bottom, her one reminder that there was still love in this room.

Edouard, pacing, kneeling, like a contractor examining the work of his crew. He didn't touch her, but she felt his breath against her exposed privates and realized he was just as close to Soren's. Still kneeling, he gave the order. *Fuck her. Slowly, at first. I'll tell you when to move faster.*

No, no, no this is all wrong. Maureen felt it and wanted to scream it, but it was too late, she'd agreed to this, and Soren, bless him, had no idea what consent meant to a man like Edouard, and was only just learning that he'd surrendered some of his own.

She sensed his hesitation. His cock tickled her, but didn't push, not at first. And then, a stir of activity, and she felt first Soren, hard and ready, penetrate her, followed by the icy sting of Edouard's flesh wrapped around the base of Soren's cock as he guided him in.

Slow. Soren's hands gripped her waist as he fell into an easy, but strained rhythm. She wished she could reach his mind, to talk to him there like she could her siblings. She needed an ally. Edouard knelt and watched, *in, out,* and then she heard the sound that still rang through her nightmares.

His zipper.

Maureen howled. Soren mistook it for pleasure and squeezed her hips, encouraged, perhaps forgetting, for a moment, that Edouard was inches away.

She was a fool. A fool for thinking this would work, but it was so much more than that! She was a fool for going forward with this marriage, for thinking she could make anything work with the man who'd raped her and taken something that could never be returned. For not taking Charles up on his offer to kill the man.

Faster, Edouard commanded, and as Soren obeyed, another familiar sound, of flesh against flesh, set to the disgusting grunts of a man who couldn't get off unless he was certain the other person would not.

Maureen's tears soiled the paper. Soren seemed to realize, finally, her agony and he stopped to check on her, but Edouard came up behind him and pushed Soren, commanding him back into motion. Moments later, she felt Soren's tears on her neck, too.

Why didn't he stop? Why didn't they run away, together, away from this?

She couldn't feel Edouard anymore. He was nearby, she could hear him, *pleasuring* himself. And then one of Soren's hands left her hips. His sigh was light, knowing, and he didn't slow his movements, but something had changed. Shifted.

Maureen turned her head, but her view was limited. She saw Soren crane his arm behind him, and there, behind him, was Edouard.

The skin-on-skin sound stopped. Soren's arm began to move, followed by a quick jerk, and then, Soren, saying, "It's okay."

Soren's arm pulled forward again and he cried as the rhythm changed, as the entire dynamic in the room altered. Edouard's own cries became animalistic, the sound of a pleasure he'd never shared and now, Maureen knew, she'd never wanted. Edouard's own rhythm, as—she understood now, in complete horror—he thrust into Soren, pushing Soren into her, one terrible motion that bound them.

With every slam of Soren against her, she felt Edouard. She felt again the things she'd prayed to God to let her forget. And when he cried out, his own completion coming first, of course, and then Soren released his own orgasm into her, Maureen had never felt so hollowed out. So lost.

Edouard left immediately after.

When he was gone, Soren took her into his arms, but she didn't want to be held. Not even by him, a victim as well, but now, also, complicit. *Why didn't you stop? Why didn't you tell him this isn't what we agreed to? How did it get this far?*

The questions weren't only for Soren, and she hated him, hated herself.

Soren sank to the floor and sobbed.

Maureen left him there, with the door open. Anyone in the staff could walk by and see him, but would they be surprised? Didn't they all know, already?

She passed Edouard in the hall on her way to her own room.

"Maureen, I'd say that went we—"

"Fuck you, for taking that from me, too," she hissed and slammed her door behind her.

"EKATHERINA LOVED YOU, AS BEST AS SHE KNEW HOW."

"I took a train to New York for you to tell me what I already know?"

Aleksei smiled, nodding. "Ekatherina, to you, is an enigma. To me, she is familiar. I see in her the other women in our family. I see in her my own *mammochka*. I see my sister. I see my uncle and cousins."

Augustus waited for the point.

"There was a darkness in Ekatherina, Augustus. It was not hers alone, and it's not her fault she was born to a people who carry it. What is it? I cannot say. Is it mental illness, or something deeper, something in the blood, something even science cannot explain? No one knows. I don't. She didn't. We talked all the time, you know."

Augustus didn't know that.

"In the beginning, she talked of this wonderful boss who looked after her. Who gave her opportunities and listened to her ideas." Aleksei grinned, his thoughts going somewhere else. "She admired you. A year younger than her, and you'd started something by yourself, ignoring those who told you that you shouldn't. Ekatherina spent most of her life ignoring those people."

"I didn't give her special treatment. She was good at what she did."

"*Da*. She was. Good enough to get first one American man to put her through school, and then another to give her a good job. She told me, too, about the necklace. What you did."

Augustus dropped his eyes. He twirled his wedding ring around his finger. It was loose now, and he didn't know why, except that he hadn't been eating the way he should. "I don't know why I did it. I saw how hard she worked, and I knew she wouldn't want a handout, but this wasn't a handout."

"It was a kindness," Aleksei said. "Though, I was surprised when she married you."

Augustus looked up.

"Ekatherina was... she was like my father, at least until he came to his senses, but there are some Soviets who do not understand what the Kremlin does to keep us safe and protect us from the dangerous influences of the western world." Aleksei gave a short laugh and gestured around. "Look, even, at this hotel. Is it necessary?"

"Necessity isn't the point. Capitalism gives us something more to strive for," Augustus said. "What is the incentive to work hard if not to earn more, produce more? Be more?"

"Capitalism is dangerous," Aleksei said, a dark cloud passing over his eyes. "But what is more dangerous is hating everything.

Ekatherina, she hated capitalism. She hated communism. She hated Russia. She hated America. She couldn't decide, and so she destroyed everything."

"You're a patriot. I see that," Augustus said. "And yet your English is way better than hers. You have almost no accent."

"It was necessary for my training. Ekatherina didn't feel it was necessary beyond what *was* necessary, do you understand? She needed English to come here, but she never wanted to forget where she came from, much as she hated it."

Augustus fell back in his chair. "You said you were surprised. When she married me."

"Don't you see? You represented what she hated more than anyone. A rich man, born into a rich family, in a rich country. A man who used his privilege and wealth to build more of the same."

"You just said she admired that."

"She admired your tenacity. She loathed your wealth."

Augustus scoffed. He looked away. "I never lived like others with money. She knew that. I never... I never stopped her from cooking her own meals, doing her own laundry. I never..."

"And that is why she loved you. But Ekatherina..." Aleksei reached into his pocket and pulled out a pack of cigarettes. "Do you mind?"

"I do mind." He nodded at his daughter.

Aleksei shook his head, but obliged. "You'll see, they'll prove the secondary smoke isn't dangerous to others. As I was saying, Ekatherina was an..." For the first time, Aleksei searched for a word. "An ana... ana..."

"Anachronism."

"Yes, yes, that is the word. An anachronism. She loved what she hated, and hated what she loved. That man. The one in Maine."

Augustus flinched.

"In you, she saw one part of her, in another, him. She didn't love him, but she loved what he represented in her very limited world. She loved that he wasn't you, because it ate her alive to love, and ate her even worse to hurt you."

"Why are you telling me this?" Augustus asked with a weary sigh.

Aleksei reached forward and tickled Ana's toes. She lit up, and they both giggled. "You can't protect this little one from the world, Augustus, but you can protect her from herself. From the same darkness that consumed her mother. Her great-grandmother. Ekatherina didn't deny her daughter because she didn't love her. She denied her because she didn't want to pass on the very thing that brought misery to her own life. But you know, I think this darkness, as they call it, isn't so impossible to escape. I think that when you surround yourself with it, it consumes you."

"What are you saying?"

"I'm saying you keep her away from us, Augustus. You raise her to believe she was loved, and that her family in Russia loves her, but you break this dangerous cycle. You do it for her, and maybe for Ekatherina, too, if there's still some love left, after it all. And you do it for you." Aleksei leaned forward. He put a hand on Augustus' knee. "Because you are a good man. That much I know from my sister. And you deserve to move on. *She*"—Aleksei pointed at Ana—"deserves a father who is happy. Who is whole. Who is not another victim of what ended things for her mother." Aleksei stood suddenly. He clasped the buttons on his suit and held out a hand to Augustus. "Send us pictures. A letter from time to time. We'll send Christmas and birthday cards and updates. That is enough."

Augustus shook his hand. As he did, he knew he'd never see the man again.

CHAPTER 20

The Persistence of Loss

"I can't believe you went," Elizabeth said. The intensity of her gaze across the table caused Augustus to drop his eyes.

"Me neither," he said and waited for the oncoming barrage of judgment.

Instead, there was only a long and uncomfortable silence.

"So," Elizabeth ventured. "Did you get what you needed?"

"I didn't know what I needed," Augustus said, as much a confession as an answer.

"But did you?"

Augustus ran his palm across his mouth, as he inhaled a deep, steadying breath. "I think so."

Elizabeth's chair screeched across the floor. "Cool. Merry Christmas. Let's get ready to head over to Charles'."

The whole family was home for Christmas, just as it had been the year before. Colleen prayed this Christmas would have all the joy of the last one, but none of the sorrow.

Charles and Cordelia no longer bothered with pretense, but

they wore their terse smiles, and their thinly disguised hatred, better than they had in the past. Lisette sat at the table this year, too, a bold move that was as much a message from Charles as it was a courtesy. She looked ready to burst, this tiny woman with her swollen belly, and at the same time, seemed so unsure of what was to come.

Augustus wasn't himself, and that was even when using his recent demeanor as the baseline. He let Irish Colleen take Ana from his arms without a fuss and hardly said a word at dinner. He smiled at all the right times, but his mind was elsewhere.

If Augustus was distant, Evangeline was more present than she'd been in years. She no longer seemed like a foreigner in her own home, but fresh and alive, in a way Colleen hadn't seen in years. She looked forward to their sister time later, where she'd learn the cause.

Maureen and her husband didn't sit together at the table. Edouard pulled a chair out next to Charles, thought better of it, and instead settled next to his mother-in-law, which, Colleen thought, wasn't much improvement. She'd talk his ear off all night. Maureen focused all her attentions on Olivia, so much so that Colleen could immediately sense something had happened. But then she smiled at Colleen, as if to say, *don't fuss about me. I don't need much.*

Elizabeth and Connor held court at the far end of the table, no longer afraid to pass glances, or even touches, as they helped move the dishes around the table. They were adults now, engaged to be married, and unafraid of their love. Colleen had never seen Lizzy so happy, and the feeling left her as sad as it did content, because, for Elizabeth, there'd never be more than moments of peace. Not with who she was.

For today, though, Elizabeth was happy.

When Colleen shared her news with the family, Noah did it with her. They took turns, alternating the message, and, together, enjoyed the congratulations and affections showered on them. Kellan, who'd joined them, and was welcome at their table for all holidays, forevermore, fed Amelia with one arm and wiped his tears with the other.

They told stories, laughed, and stuffed themselves silly. They were a family, for one night. A family that was connected, not because of change, but choice.

When Colleen went to sleep that night, belly full of food and heart full of love, she said a silent prayer, thanking God for a Christmas she'd want to remember in the days to come.

THE NEXT MORNING, AUGUSTUS KISSED HIS DAUGHTER on the cheek and wished her a happy first birthday.

"We're going to see Mama," he said and bundled her into her winter suit.

THE DESCHANEL TOMB WAS LOCATED IN SQUARE THREE of Lafayette Cemetery No. 1, at the corner of Sixth and Prytania. Even in the winter the large lot was shaded by bowing oaks and steadfast magnolia. The greenspace, lined with benches, was frosted over. It was a cold morning, colder than it had been.

The tomb itself was one of the largest in the cemetery, four times the size of the other large tombs. Names, inscriptions, poems, and psalms covering almost every inch, with the center slab housing the names of the heir and his line. Angels danced around the spires topping the tomb, wearing the soft patina of time.

Our darling Madeline, aged seventeen years.

August Deschanel, he died as he lived, an honorable man.

Ekatherina, beloved wife, doting mother.

Augustus dropped onto a concrete bench. It was freezing, and his pants dampened from the overnight frost, but he hardly noticed. Ana's pale face flushed in the cold, so he settled her hood around her more neatly. She regarded him with her mother's eyes.

He looked away from her and focused ahead. He started talking, before he could find reason to convince himself to leave without saying what he had to say.

"Ekatherina, I'm sorry this is the first time I've been here since the service. I tried to come, for Ana, just as I've done everything else for her, but somewhere, deep down, I knew that when I did come see you, it would have to be for me."

Augustus bowed over his knees. "I've had so much *anger* since you left us. It's built up inside of me and I tried to turn it into something productive, God knows. I tried to reverse it and give all my energy to raising our daughter, but I hardly remember anything from her first year because I spent it focused more on the past than the future."

Tears pricked his eyes. Ana cooed in her stroller, but if he looked at her again, before he finished, he might lose his courage. And for her, he had to expel his own darkness.

"I will raise our Ana because I choose to, Ekatherina. I will give her what you would not. And I will forgive you, so that I can raise her without this anger, this swell of rage and resentment that I've let bury and fester inside of me, and change me into a man I hardly recognize."

Soft, damp pricks of rain peppered his raincoat. He pulled the cover over Ana's stroller. He reached underneath her seat and pulled out a wreath of chamomile, roses, and lilies. He had it made from her favorite flowers from her days in Russia. He didn't know she had a favorite flower, but the packet Aleksei left with him, titled *Things Anasofiya Might Like to Know One Day*, had a lot of information about Ekatherina that surprised him and reminded him how little he actually knew her.

"I'll be back, but not for me next time. For Ana, who deserves to believe she was loved by the person who should have loved her most in the world."

For Ana, Augustus would craft the most effective illusion he'd ever crafted. He'd shrug off the persistence of loss and embrace whatever arrived in its place.

For Ana.

Epilogue: Irish Colleen and the Seven

Colleen Deschanel, known as Irish Colleen to her family and friends, walked past the faces of her seven children, and four grandchildren, as she did every night of her life. Soon, Charles would bring a daughter to the family, and Colleen, a son.

But there was one more grandchild. One that would never be spoken of in this household, in her lifetime.

That Irish Colleen knew about Catherine's hidden delivery in Boston and neither her husband nor lover knew a thing, was shocking, but a blessing. Irish Colleen came to the information by interpreting the world around her, as she had always done. Her children accused her of being a secret witch, but it didn't take a witch to decipher Catherine's frantic phone calls to Colleen, Colleen's furtive glances. Her trips to Boston, which weren't a secret when the receipts came in the mail.

But, she would never, no matter how she wished to hold her sweet granddaughter, ever tell a soul. She'd be content with the few minutes she got at picnics and get-togethers, doting over the child of a family friend.

She had to be, or it would tear two families apart.

Augustus was changed. It started on Christmas, but when she

saw him earlier that night, on New Year's Eve, he had a glow in his cheeks that hadn't been there since Madeline was still alive. He set Ana on the carpet to play with Olivia, and even let her out of his sight, joining his mother in the kitchen for a cup of tea.

When she asked how he was doing, he said, *I'll be fine, Mama.*

Colleen was about to give her a second grandchild, and though Irish Colleen sensed some hesitation in her daughter, it was only her old self, dusting off the cobwebs to remind her she needed something to worry about. But she also saw a miracle: Colleen fighting it, with Noah by her side and at her back. If there was such a thing as a perfect man for Colleen, it was Noah Jameson.

Kellan Jameson was a fine man, too. He carried a great burden with him, always, but he'd done his penance. And she didn't mind him coming over, helping around the house, joining her for the occasional meal. It had been quite some time since someone wanted to befriend her for who she was, and not what a connection to her could do for them.

Evangeline had also found her peace, though in what, she was reluctant to say. She conveyed only that, when the time came, she'd tell them what she was working on. *It's a good thing,* she insisted, when Irish Colleen trained her concerned eyes on her unpredictable daughter. *Maybe the best thing I've ever done. Or will do.*

Maureen's marriage was more complicated now than it ever was. As she often did, Irish Colleen wished she could find a way to tell her how alike they were. How she might be surprised at what could be understood between them, not only as mother-daughter but as women who had both experienced things no one else could comprehend. Experienced them and found ways to survive them.

Elizabeth lived with Augustus now full-time, but she'd stayed the night for New Year's, wanting to spend time with Colleen before she flew back to Scotland. Irish Colleen went to say good night to her, but Elizabeth wasn't alone.

"He gave me this," Elizabeth said.

"Lizzy!" Colleen cried. "What a beautiful locket. Oh, look, it's the two of you inside."

"Yeah," Elizabeth said.

"What's wrong? You don't like it?"

"Colleen, I've been carrying around this great burden for so long and I have to share it with someone. But if I share it with you, you'll hate me."

"I could never hate you, Lizzy. Not for anything."

Irish Colleen knew she should leave, but was rooted in place, by both fear and curiosity.

Elizabeth's next words came out through jagged breaths. "I've seen my future."

"But... how?"

"Through Connor. I saw my future in his future."

"But isn't that..."

"Good? Some of it. Some of it is wonderful. There will be children someday, Colleen. Two of them. A boy and a girl."

"I don't understand. What—"

"One of them will die, Colleen. And so will I. I'll bury my daughter, and then I'll die before my son is old enough to have his own children. And Connor will never be the same after."

Irish Colleen clasped both hands over her mouth to keep from crying out.

"Lizzy... maybe it's wrong, maybe—"

"No, Colleen. It's not wrong. You know it's not wrong. It's never wrong." Elizabeth's sobs pierced Irish Colleen right through the heart. "But I saw something else tonight, when Connor gave this to me."

"Tell me."

"I had a vision of my son holding this necklace one day, a day after I'm gone. And then I saw him save our family. And I knew... I knew, finally, that my decision to live wasn't about me at all, Colleen. It's not about my suffering, or even my joy. I know now that I was born to produce a child who would one day save us all."

Colleen's next words were unintelligible.

"It's okay, Leena. I've made peace with it. Connor has, in his own way. You will, too. But you're the leader of this family now, and you need to know how important Tristan is. Because I saw a day where your choice to believe in him is what will lead him down the right path. The path that leads to our salvation."

"Of course, of course I'll believe in him, he's your son, and—"

"Hope, Colleen. You asked me what I saw in my vision. I saw hope."

Four years. How much can a person change, in four years? How much does the world change, in four years?

The series concludes in 1980.

Also by Sarah M. Cradit

KINGDOM OF THE WHITE SEA

Kingdom of the White Sea Trilogy

The Kingless Crown

The Broken Realm

The Hidden Kingdom

The Book of All Things

The Raven and the Rush

The Sylvan and the Sand

The Altruist and the Assassin

The Melody and the Master

The Claw and the Crowned

THE SAGA OF CRIMSON & CLOVER

The House of Crimson and Clover Series

The Storm and the Darkness

Shattered

The Illusions of Eventide

Bound

Midnight Dynasty

Asunder

Empire of Shadows

Myths of Midwinter

The Hinterland Veil

The Secrets Amongst the Cypress

Within the Garden of Twilight

House of Dusk, House of Dawn

Midnight Dynasty Series

A Tempest of Discovery

A Storm of Revelations

A Torrent of Deceit

The Seven Series

1970

1972

1973

1974

1975

1976

1980

Vampires of the Merovingi Series

The Island

and more

The Dusk Trilogy

St. Charles at Dusk: The Story of Oz and Adrienne

Flourish: The Story of Anne Fontaine

Banshee: The Story of Giselle Deschanel

Crimson & Clover Stories

Surrender: The Story of Oz and Ana

Shame: The Story of Jonathan St. Andrews

Fire & Ice: The Story of Remy & Fleur

Dark Blessing: The Landry Triplets

Pandora's Box: The Story of Jasper & Pandora

The Menagerie: Oriana's Den of Iniquities

A Band of Heather: The Story of Colleen and Noah

The Ephemeral: The Story of Autumn & Gabriel

Bayou's Edge: The Landry Triplets

For more information, and exciting bonus material, visit www.sarahmcradit.com

The Family

Deschanel Family (Line of August)

The Deschanel (*pronounced Day-shah-nell*) family are the line of heirs of the great Charles Deschanel of France, who settled the Deschanel dynasty in Louisiana in 1844. All current day descendants of this original Charles are either of the line of August or Blanche. Deschanels are of the line of August, and all others (Fontenots, Broussards, Guidrys, etc.) come from Blanche. August, with his wife "Irish" Colleen Brady, had seven children: Charles, Augustus, Colleen, Madeline, Evangeline, Maureen, and Elizabeth. Madeline, their fourth child, tragically passed in an automobile accident on Christmas morning, 1970.

Irish Colleen was August's second wife. His first, Eliza, he married for love, but she was unable to bear children and eventually passed away from cancer.

The rights of inheritance of the Deschanels follow the tradition of the eldest son, so Charles, son of August, is the current heir.

August (1905-1961) & "Irish" Colleen Brady (1932-)

Charles b. 1950 (m. Cordelia Hendrickson b. 1951)
Nicolas b. 1975

Augustus b. 1951 (m. Ekatherina Vasilyeva b. 1950)
Anasofiya b. 1975

Colleen b. 1952 (m. Noah Jameson b. 1950)

Madeline 1953-1970

Evangeline b. 1954

Maureen b. 1956 (m. Edouard Blanchard b. 1935)
Olivia b. 1975

Elizabeth b. 1959

Deschanel-Broussard Family (Line of Blanche)

The Deschanel-Broussard family (*pronounced Brew-sard*), are cousins of the Deschanel family, equal in wealth and prestige. Where the Deschanels are descendants of the line of August, the Broussards are descendants of the line of Blanche. Claudius Broussard is Blanche's third husband, and the children from this union are considered her most favored. She also has a son by her second husband, Johnson Guidry, but her relationship with Pierce is fractured.

Blanche did not have children by her first husband, Ellis Kenner. Both Ellis Kenner and Johnson Guidry died of "mysterious circumstances."

Blanche Deschanel (b. 1906) & Johnson Guidry (1890-1930)
Pierce b. 1926

& Claudius Broussard (b. 1900)
Eugenia b. 1940
Pierce b. 1926
Cassius b. 1942
Wyatt (1943-1955)
Noble (1944-1955)

Guidry Family (Line of Blanche)

The Guidry family are those descended from Pierce Guidry, first son of Blanche Deschanel-Broussard. Although the first son is the heir on the Deschanel side, Blanche does not recognize Pierce as her heir. Instead, she sees her second child and eldest daughter, Eugenia Fontenot, as her heir. Pierce represents his line of the family as one of the seven Deschanel Magi Collective Council. His two daughters, Pansy and Kitty, are also on the Council.

Of Pierce's children, only Pansy, so far, is married.

The Guidrys, for no reason other than Blanche's disdain for her second husband, Johnson, are considered the black sheep of the clan.

Pierce Guidry (b. 1926) & Winnifred Babin (b. 1926)
Pansy b. 1949
Alton b. 1950
Kitty b. 1954

Pansy b. 1949 m. Placide Lafont b. 1945
Rex b. 1973

Fontenot Family (Line of Blanche)

The Fontenot family are those descended from Eugenia Broussard-Fontenot, second daughter of Blanche Deschanel-Broussard. Although Eugenia is a second child, and a daughter to boot, Blanche recognizes Eugenia as her heir. Eugenia is married to Wallace Fontenot, and they have three sons. Eugenia represents her line of the family as one of the seven Deschanel Magi Collective Council.

The Fontenots are well-respected in the community, with a similar prestige as their Deschanel cousins.

Eugenia Broussard (b. 1940) & Wallace Fontenot (b. 1939)

Luther b. 1962
Llewellyn b. 1963
Lowell b. 1964

Broussard Family (Line of Blanche)

The Broussard family are those descended from Cassius, third child and second son of Blanche Deschanel-Broussard. Cassius is married to Helene Barrow, and they have two children, a son and a daughter. Cassius represents his line of the family as one of the seven Deschanel Magi Collective Council.

The Broussards, like the Fontenots, are well-respected in the community, with a similar prestige as their Deschanel cousins.

Cassius Broussard (b. 1942) & Helene Barrow (b. 1944)

Jasper b. 1963
Imogen b. 1965

Sullivan Family

The Sullivans are one of the oldest and most trusted families in New Orleans. A family of attorneys, a majority of Sullivans, most notably males until recently, join the family law firm, Sullivan & Associates, which has been a New Orleans staple since 1839. The family came up through the ranks, by their bootstraps, with humble beginnings as Irish immigrant laborers. The Sullivans are both the attorneys and friends of the Deschanel Family. Like the Deschanels, the designation of heir follows the eldest son, and so Colin Sullivan Sr. is considered the head of the family. His father, Patrick, still lives, but in quiet retirement.

Colin Sullivan Sr. (b. 1932) & Josephine Bartleby (b. 1931)

Colin Jr. b. 1950 (m. Catherine Connelly b. 1948)
Rory b. 1952 (m. Carolina Percy b. 1953)
Patrick b. 1953
Chelsea b. 1956

Sullivan & Associates

Sullivan & Associates is a family-owned law firm, and one of the oldest and most trusted in New Orleans, founded in 1839 by Aidan Sullivan. Comprised mostly of Sullivans, the firm is considered something of a birthright for any Sullivans looking to go into law. They have represented the Deschanel interests for over a century. Charles Deschanel's best friend, Colin Sullivan Jr., as well as Colin's two brothers, Rory and Patrick, all plan to join the family firm one day. Colin Sullivan Sr. is the current Senior Partner, following the retirement of his father, Patrick. Colin Sr. and his brothers, Jerome and Jamie, are the figureheads of the firm.

Homes & Properties

Oak Haven

The old Victorian mansion Irish Colleen and seven used to live in, on Chestnut and Sixth in the Garden District, just beyond Lafayette Cemetery No. 1. Although there are larger (Magnolia Grace) and more storied (Ophélie) homes in the family possession, August Deschanel chose this particular property to raise his family in with the thought of giving them a more "normal" upbringing than he had.

The Gardens

The colossal mansion and family seat of the Deschanels at Jackson Ave., taking up an entire square block between Coliseum and Prytania in the Garden District. The Gardens also houses the cavernous chambers where the Deschanel Magi Collective and the Collective Council meet to discuss family business. The architectural style of the estate is Italianate, and the most notable feature is the extensive, exotic garden wrapping around the property, shielding the home from outside view. Ophelia Deschanel occupied this house for many years, as the long-standing Magistrate. This house is now Colleen's, as the next Magistrate of the Deschanel Magi Collective.

Ophélie

A large plantation and surrounding lands purchased by Charles Deschanel I, built in 1844, and currently occupied intermittently by the Deschanel family. Charles will inherit the property as the heir to the estate. Located near Vacherie, an hour west of New Orleans, the Greek Revival ivory mansion on the Mississippi River is secluded from the road by gates and foliage. The estate has forty-five rooms and large ornate gardens, as well as two hundred outbuildings from when the property was a working plantation. Charles, as the heir, has inherited this property.

Magnolia Grace

A beautiful, traditional Greek Revival mansion in the Garden District that once belonged to Fitz Deschanel (the second son of Charles I), and has ever since been passed down through the second sons. Augustus Deschanel inherited this property, which is located on Prytania, near Eighth.

Deschanel Media Group

The brainchild of Augustus Deschanel, who had dreamed of starting his own company since he was a young boy. The company's vision is a magazine for locals, which both catered to the elites but also offered an opportunity for aspiring writers to get their short stories published and in front of potential patrons.

Femme Forte

A sprawling Northshore mansion along Lake Pontchartrain, considered the birthright of Blanche and her descendants. The property will be inherited by Eugenia Fontenot, her favorite child.

Blanchard House

An old, esteemed mansion along St. Charles Avenue in the

Garden District, passed down through the Blanchard family over many generations. Though an exceptional home, Edouard keeps it dark and in some degree of disrepair.

Weatherly Estate

The vast, columned Uptown home of Daniel Weatherly Sr., gifted for his patronage of Tulane. His son, Dan Jr., is a good friend of Charles Deschanel. The estate is located near the sister universities of Tulane and Loyola, by the Ursuline's Academy.

Also by Sarah M. Cradit

KINGDOM OF THE WHITE SEA

<u>Kingdom of the White Sea Trilogy</u>

The Kingless Crown

The Broken Realm

The Hidden Kingdom

<u>The Book of All Things</u>

Blackwood Cycle

The Raven and the Rush

The Poison and the Paladin

Southerlands Cycle

The Sylvan and the Sand

The Flame and the Forsaken

Guardians Cycle

The Altruist and the Assassin

The Belle and the Blackbird

Darkwood Cycle

The Melody and the Master

The Hand and the Heart

Sceptre Cycle

The Claw and the Crowned

The Duke and the Disciple

THE SAGA OF CRIMSON & CLOVER

<u>The House of Crimson and Clover Series</u>

The Storm and the Darkness

Shattered

The Illusions of Eventide

Bound

Midnight Dynasty

Asunder

Empire of Shadows

Myths of Midwinter

The Hinterland Veil

The Secrets Amongst the Cypress

Within the Garden of Twilight

House of Dusk, House of Dawn

<u>Midnight Dynasty Series</u>

A Tempest of Discovery

A Storm of Revelations

A Torrent of Deceit

<u>The Seven Series</u>

Nineteen Seventy

Nineteen Seventy-Two

Nineteen Seventy-Three

Nineteen Seventy-Four

Nineteen Seventy-Five

Nineteen Seventy-Six

Nineteen Eighty

Vampires of the Merovingi Series

The Island

and more

The Dusk Trilogy

St. Charles at Dusk: The Story of Oz and Adrienne

Flourish: The Story of Anne Fontaine

Banshee: The Story of Giselle Deschanel

Crimson & Clover Stories

Available as a single collection, The Shorts

Surrender: The Story of Oz and Ana

Shame: The Story of Jonathan St. Andrews

Fire & Ice: The Story of Remy & Fleur

Dark Blessing: The Landry Triplets

Pandora's Box: The Story of Jasper & Pandora

The Menagerie: Oriana's Den of Iniquities

A Band of Heather: The Story of Colleen and Noah

The Ephemeral: The Story of Autumn & Gabriel

Bayou's Edge: The Landry Triplets

For more information, and exciting bonus material, visit www.sarahmcradit.com

About the Author

Sarah is the USA Today and International Bestselling Author of over forty contemporary and epic fantasy stories, and the creator of the Kingdom of the White Sea and Saga of Crimson & Clover universes.

Born a geek, Sarah spends her time crafting rich and multilayered worlds, obsessing over history, playing her retribution paladin (and sometimes destruction warlock), and settling provocative Tolkien debates, such as why the Great Eagles are not Gandalf's personal taxi service. Passionate about travel, she's been to over twenty countries collecting sparks of inspiration, and is always planning her next adventure.

Sarah and her husband live in a beautiful corner of SE Pennsylvania with their three tiny benevolent pug dictators.

www.sarahmcradit.com